HERMANN HESSE (1   Calw, a small
southern German town in the northern Black Forest, in July
1877. He was the son and grandson of a family of strict Pietist
missionaries, a heritage that affected him deeply throughout his
life. His grandparents had spent decades of their lives on the
Malabar coast of India, where his mother also lived and worked.
By the time Hesse was born, however, the family had settled in
Calw, though he spent part of his early childhood in a dormitory
for missionaries' children in Basel, Switzerland, the main seat of
their movement, where his father was teaching. Later, back in
Germany, he went through another period of institutionalized
living in a Protestant boarding school housed in an old monastery not far from his home. His escape from the school at fifteen
years of age became the subject of his novel *Beneath the Wheel*.
Both experiences fortified his distaste for authority and his celebration of the individual.

In 1895, at age eighteen, Hermann Hesse struck out for himself by taking work in a Basel bookstore. It took him nine more
years of writing, however, to establish himself with his first full-
length novel, *Peter Camenzind* (1904), followed by *Beneath the
Wheel* (1906), *Gertrud* (1910), and *Rosshalde* (1914), as well as
a wealth of short fiction, including *Knulp* (1915). He married
Maria Bernoulli of a prominent Swiss family and lived with her
and their three sons on the shore of Lake Constance in
Switzerland.

A significant change in Hesse's life occurred with the outbreak of World War I. He spent the war years in Bern,
Switzerland, working with an agency under the auspices of the
Red Cross, supplying books and other amenities to German
prisoners of war. After the war and a psychological crisis, his
marriage shattered, and Hesse removed himself to Montagnola,
a small town in Italian-speaking Switzerland. There—in the relative peace of rural surroundings, interrupted only occasionally
by forays into the urban centers of Zurich and Basel—he created
his best-known work: *Siddhartha* (1922), *Steppenwolf* (1927),
Narcissus and Goldmund (1930), *Journey to the East* (1932),

and *The Glass Bead Game* (1943). Remarried in his later years to Ninon Ausländer, a Jewish immigrant from Romania who inspired and sustained him in the face of his failing eyesight, he lived out his life in the seclusion of Montagnola. He received many important honors, including the Nobel Prize for Literature in 1946, and died in 1962 soon after his eighty-fifth birthday.

Hesse's entire life—from his resistance to authority in his young years to the mature writer's insistence on individuality in a mass culture—was devoted to those of his readers (of all ages, but especially the young) who search for wholeness and authenticity in the face of the recurrent crises that have shaped our time.

DAMION SEARLS writes fiction, criticism, and biography, and has translated many classic twentieth-century authors, including Proust, Rilke, Robert Walser, Nescio, Thomas Bernhard, and Christa Wolf. His translation of Hans Keilson's *Comedy in a Minor Key* was a *New York Times* Notable Book and a National Book Critics Circle Award finalist. Searls received a Guggenheim Fellowship in 2012; he lives in Brooklyn, New York.

JAMES FRANCO is an actor, director, author, and visual artist. His film appearances include *Milk*, *Pineapple Express*, *Howl*, and *127 Hours*, which earned him an Academy Award nomination. Franco is the author of the story collection *Palo Alto*, and his writing has been published in *Esquire*, *Vanity Fair*, *n+1*, the *Wall Street Journal*, and *McSweeney's*. Franco's art has been exhibited throughout the world, including at the Museum of Contemporary Art in Los Angeles, the Museum of Modern Art's PS1 in New York, the Clocktower Gallery in New York, and the Peres Projects in Berlin.

RALPH FREEDMAN, professor emeritus of comparative literature at Princeton University, is acclaimed for his biographies *Hermann Hesse: Pilgrim of Crisis* and *Life of a Poet: Rainer Maria Rilke*.

C2

HERMANN HESSE

Demian

THE STORY OF
EMIL SINCLAIR'S YOUTH

Translated by
DAMION SEARLS

Foreword by
JAMES FRANCO

Introduction by
RALPH FREEDMAN

PENGUIN BOOKS

Grand Forks Public Library

PENGUIN BOOKS
Published by the Penguin Group
Penguin Group (USA) Inc., 375 Hudson Street,
New York, New York 10014, USA

USA | Canada | UK | Ireland | Australia | New Zealand | India | South Africa | China
Penguin Books Ltd, Registered Offices: 80 Strand, London WC2R 0RL, England
For more information about the Penguin Group visit penguin.com

This translation first published in Penguin Books 2013

Translation copyright © Damion Searls, 2013
Introduction copyright © Ralph Freedman, 2013
Foreword copyright © Whose Dog RU International, Inc., 2013

All rights reserved. No part of this product may be reproduced, scanned, or distributed in any
printed or electronic form without permission. Please do not participate in or encourage piracy of
copyrighted materials in violation of the author's rights. Purchase only authorized editions.

Originally published in German by S. Fischer Verlag, Berlin, 1919

LIBRARY OF CONGRESS CATALOGING-IN-PUBLICATION DATA
Hesse, Hermann, 1877–1962.
[Demian. English]
Demian : the story of Emil Sinclair's youth / Hermann Hesse ; translated by Damion Searls ;
foreword by James Franco ; introduction by Ralph Freedman.
pages cm.—(Penguin Classics)
Includes bibliographical references.
ISBN 978-0-14-310678-4
1. Young men—Germany—Fiction. 2. Germany—Social conditions—1918–1933—Fiction.
I. Searls, Damion, translator. II. Title.
PT2617.E85D413 2013
833'.912—dc23
2013006661

Printed in the United States of America
13th Printing

Set in Adobe Sabon

Contents

DEMIAN

Foreword

MY FRIEND *DEMIAN*

I remember reading *Demian* for the first time. It was the beginning of summer. I had turned nineteen in April, and I was working at a café on the UCLA campus, selling deli sandwiches, microwaved pizza, cheap Mexican hash, and glistening Chinese food. I had spent the previous school year studying English literature but had recently taken the plunge into the raging sea of film acting and was freshly making my way through the tide pools of acting school. I had not auditioned for the UCLA theater program and thus had been forced to take classes in the Valley, and just before the spring quarter at UCLA had ended I decided to devote myself full-time to acting. My parents didn't object, saying only that they would support me as long as I studied at the university, but if I wanted to be an artist I had to find my own way.

Working at the North Campus eatery, I was serving the students who once had been my classmates. My boss was a graduate student with a shaved head except in two spots that he dyed red and gelled into six-inch horns. I'll call him Bill. I remember liking Bill if only because he was closer to my age than any boss I'd ever had, but he was still a boss. I was working to support my dream (one of a few) to become a film actor, and my employer looked like the devil.

On my breaks I read plays by O'Neill, Tennessee Williams, Shaw, Ibsen, Chekhov, and anyone else who might help me understand my chosen profession. It turned out that the grinding aspect of the job was not Bill's constant watch as I loaded meat and mustard on sandwiches or scooped chiles rellenos from the tin, depending on the day of the week; it was the boredom.

I know now that I learned much about responsibility, dedication, and service from that humble job, but back then I had dreams of grandeur. I had left school in order to become the best actor in the world, and here I was, back on campus serving the very people who had been inviting me to frat parties a few months prior. I seemed to have taken five steps backward, and the fact that I had left a top-rated university to join an army of hopefuls trying to break into a famously competitive industry often seemed like a fool's quest.

On the wall next to the pizza service section was a framed photo of an elderly Marlon Brando being led by a man in a suit and a football helmet through a throng of photographers and gawkers. I'm pretty sure it was taken around the time of Brando's son's murder trial, but it inspired me as I served the slop: Brando was the pinnacle of film acting, and his picture was a reminder of the great tradition I hoped to be a part of.

After a couple of months I started reading *Demian*. I'm not sure if there was a connection, but one day, without warning, I hung up my apron and walked out the back, never to return. I had planned to work that day, so once I'd taken my exit, I didn't know where to go. With *Demian* folded in my pocket, I headed into Westwood, full of passion because of what I had done. On the edge of campus I ran into one of my former classmates, a girl I once had flirted with, sunning herself on the grass. I told her what had happened, but it didn't seem to register. I felt as if I had taken another step away from a conformist life and another step toward artistic freedom, but, talking to her, I sounded to myself like an immature kid who had quit his job.

At a café I jumped back into reading *Demian* and felt as if I was understood again. Emil Sinclair, the narrator, is also on a search. His vacillation between good and bad, between expected pursuits and his own artistic path, seemed to mirror mine. Like so many young people in the ninety years since the novel's publication, I felt as if Hermann Hesse was describing my own interior and exterior struggles. Sinclair had Demian to help guide him, but I had yet to find my artistic mentor. Instead I had the book.

Demian became my Demian, a voice I could listen to and contemplate as I tried to find my way from childhood to adulthood and into the world of art. Of course there were many turns in the road ahead—I would get a job at McDonald's, get work as an actor, grow to hate much of the work I did, expand my artistic horizons (Hesse became not just a writer but also a celebrated painter)—but reading *Demian* was an important step in the direction of a life that resonated with my ideals.

JAMES FRANCO

Introduction

*New readers are advised that this introduction
makes details of the plot explicit.*

It is a signal honor to introduce Hermann Hesse's *Demian* to a contemporary audience, since it means following in the footsteps of no less a predecessor than Thomas Mann, who wrote in April 1947, "For me, [Hesse's] life, with its roots in native German romanticism, for all its strange individualism, its now humorously petulant and now mystically yearning estrangement from the world and the times, belongs to the highest and purest spiritual aspirations and labors of our epoch."[1] This statement accurately describes the achievement of Hesse, whose vision appealed not only to the generation of young men who survived World War I, but also to the counterculture of the 1960s and '70s in America and Europe.[2]

This new translation returns *Demian* to our consciousness as a welcome face we had almost forgotten. Hesse's later works like *Siddhartha* and *Steppenwolf* have long since become part of our lives, but *Demian*, the novel that blazed the trail for those later works, has unjustly dropped into the background. As *Demian* and its stirring message once led readers into a new world of creation, Hesse's vision is again reaching out to another generation searching for meaning in an age of anxiety and war.

I

On the surface, *Demian* appears to be a simple novel of education.

Young Emil Sinclair is acutely aware of two forces in the

world—the good and the evil. He is rescued from the control of a neighborhood bully by a classmate, Max Demian, who becomes his mentor. Demian leads Sinclair to various symbols that accompany him for life—including a sparrow hawk carved above Sinclair's front door. Away at boarding school, Sinclair drinks heavily and neglects his studies, but a beautiful young woman he sees in a park transforms his life, even though he never meets her. Sinclair discovers painting as a means of expressing his inner turmoil. He paints the woman's portrait and recognizes her resemblance to Demian, his childhood mentor and savior. He next paints the image of the hawk emerging from its egg, and of Jacob wrestling with the angel—portraits of his own struggle for self-realization. He learns of a Persian god, Abraxas, who incarnates the universe, including good and evil, light and dark, masculine and feminine. The musician and theologian Pistorius teaches him more about Abraxas—and about himself. Sinclair transcends this mentor and finds Demian again, now with Demian's mother, Eve. At the outbreak of World War I, Demian and Sinclair become soldiers. The dying Demian passes on his legacy of enlightenment to the severely wounded Sinclair.

Delving into this story, we will encounter Hesse's projection of both an individual and a generation against the backdrop of impending disaster.

2

Demian is at the same time the story of a youth and the history of the emotional crisis and intellectual evolution of a man around forty. In writing this novel, Hesse balanced the presentation of his own individual experience with the portrayal of universal problems. We respond to this dual effort even today, because, in the issues the novel raises—good versus evil, war and its aftermath—we recognize that our own relative safety is likewise projected against the monstrous deaths of others.

In one of the first sentences of the book, Hesse states his position on personal versus universal experience. "Novelists when they write novels," he says, "tend to take an almost god-like attitude toward their subject, pretending to a total comprehension of the story, a man's life, which they can therefore recount as God Himself might, nothing standing between them and the naked truth, the entire story meaningful in every detail."[3] This, he declares, he cannot do. Instead of presenting an invented and therefore a mendacious work about imagined people, he wants to write a "real story about a real, unique living person." Through Hesse's new artistry, this person became by extension the author himself, yet "objectified" in an attempt to come to grips with evil in man, in society, and, of course, the cataclysmic evil of war.

Composed under great personal stress, *Demian* was published in 1919. It appeared first in monthly installments from February to April in the literary journal *Die Neue Rundschau*, then in book form in June of that year. Both times it was published under the pseudonym of its protagonist, Emil Sinclair.

Pretending to be Sinclair had the great advantage for Hesse of assuring readers, many of whom were returning soldiers, that such a young writer—much like themselves—actually existed. These soldiers came home defeated, having survived the horrors of trench warfare only to confront humiliation, the miseries of revolution, and a nationwide depression. They were seeking a way out, and Emil Sinclair's story provided provisional answers.

Another reason why Hesse published the novel under a pseudonym was more deeply personal. He evidently wished to signify that he had embarked on a new life. Whatever his motives, Hesse was so successful that *Demian* won the notable Fontane Prize as a first novel (though in reality it was his fifth). The prize, named for the popular novelist Theodor Fontane (1819–1898), gave further proof that "Emil Sinclair" was a beginning author who promised great distinction.

But something about this manuscript made certain prominent people doubt that Sinclair was really the author. By all accounts, Hesse's publisher, Samuel Fischer, initially accepted the pseudonym as real, although Fischer's wife, Hedwig, was among the first to guess the author's true identity. The matter was officially brought to an end by Eduard Korrodi, the editor for literature and the arts at the *Neue Zürcher Zeitung*, who revealed the truth in an open letter "To Hermann Hesse" on July 4, 1920.[4] It must have been with considerable regret that Hesse had to return the prize when his authorship was revealed.

Demian's reception was an instant success and continued to be so despite the revelation of its authorship, in large part because the book is a reflection of its time, embodying both order and underlying chaos in a society whose complacency had been violently disrupted by World War I. Although Sinclair and the avid readers who identified with him were more than twenty years younger than Hesse was, Hesse had understood and expressed their feelings and frustrations. Oddly, though, the war itself is hardly mentioned except in the foreword and the final chapter.

Still, it is a war novel. How can that be?

3

The answer lies within Hesse's life and his continuing intimacy with his art. *Demian* is not precisely *about* World War I, but is a product of and a reaction to the war.[5] Hesse's earlier novels, like *Beneath the Wheel* (1906), dramatized the failure of the social order in education, and his *Rosshalde* (1914) dramatized the same failure in the artist's struggle with the institution of marriage. But, at the end of the old century and the beginning of the new one, Hesse's readers knew him mainly as a poet in prose, the romantic wanderer through nature like the vagabond Knulp in a small book of that name, which Hesse published in 1915.

Then came the Great War that changed the world, and at the war's end came *Demian*, which addressed a new wave of readers. Hesse's postwar fiction, like *Klingsor's Last Summer* (1920) or *Siddhartha* (1922), emerged from the shadowy period in history just before the end of the war and during the precarious peace that followed. *Demian* ushered in this new

era in Hesse's writings, a decisive turn, anticipating his best
novels of the later years, like *Steppenwolf* (1927), *Narcissus
and Goldmund* (1930), and *The Glass Bead Game* (1943).

Like most of Hesse's books, *Demian* is deeply but not slav-
ishly autobiographical. As an expression of his antiestablish-
ment views, Hesse draws on material from his own life but
transforms it into a new vision. He probably named Emil Sinclair after Isaac von Sinclair, a nineteenth-century revolutionary once accused of high treason, and a friend of the poet
Friedrich Hölderlin, whom Hesse admired.[6] He also used "Sinclair" as the pen name for a series of political and literary
pamphlets he published.

Demian most closely links Hesse's life and art in its account
of its hero's young years. A glance at Hesse's childhood in a
strict Pietist household, where he felt isolated as a rebel, suggests that with *Demian* he sought to exorcise a demon in himself. Sinclair's family in a small-town home with a fair but
strict father, a protective and overpowering mother, and two
prim sisters reflects Hesse's own childhood in the Black Forest
town of Calw. This was also the region where the young writer
went to boarding school and later to the university. Like Hesse's,
Sinclair's adolescent years during the fin de siècle and the early
years of the twentieth century were rife with excess, alcohol,
and arrogant behavior.

The time of *Demian*'s gestation and its date of publication
correspond to Hesse's struggle to free himself from his marriage and family in order to strike out on his own. The third
year of the war, 1916, saw the death of Hesse's father and the
growing mental illness of his wife, Maria Bernoulli, or Mia.
Under this pressure, Hesse suffered a deepening depression of
his own. His novel successfully embodies both the crises of
war and those within himself, and the emergence of both
Hesse and Europe from one phase of life to a new one.

In 1917, Hesse's youngest son, Martin, became seriously ill,
and Hesse himself suffered a nervous breakdown. He entered
Sonnmatt, a sanatorium near Lucerne. In a letter to an old
friend, Helene Welti, he described succinctly his state of mind
at that time: "I'm suffering from the growth of a crisis, where

the physical aspect is only of negligible though of symbolic importance . . . partly an inner disharmony, which has grown in me for years but which now, somehow, demands a solution, if carrying on is to have any meaning at all."[7] Hesse, as is often noted, stands out as the first major writer to have been psychoanalyzed. As a key to his inner self and to the work that reflects it, psychoanalysis offers a useful perspective.

At Sonnmatt, Hesse was treated by the perceptive analyst Dr. Josef Bernhard Lang, a disciple of C. G. Jung's. A near-mythical meeting brought together the thirty-three-year-old analyst and the well-known writer of thirty-nine. Their therapy took place in the extremely personal atmosphere typical of the early years of psychoanalysis—an analysis that consisted of twelve sessions lasting up to three hours each, and, after Hesse's release from the sanatorium, continuing with fifty more sessions in Dr. Lang's apartment in Lucerne.

This experience was crucial for *Demian* and its daring penetration of the unconscious. Hesse came well prepared. In 1918, he had written an essay entitled "Artists and Psychoanalysis," insisting that the artist's "search for psychological causes in memories, dreams, and associations, retains as its permanent gain what may be called the inner relationship *to his own unconscious*."[8] Hesse welcomed Freud's concept of "sublimation," then becoming known, a way of displacing feelings by substituting artistic creation for them. Through his growing friendship with Dr. Lang, Hesse also assimilated Jung's view that the content of the individual's unconscious is an expression of a "collective" unconscious, determined by the memories and symbols of a given culture. Although Hesse remained sympathetic to Freud's individual approach, the dreams that fill the pages of *Demian* are subject primarily to a Jungian interpretation. In fact, the role of J. B. Lang in Hesse's life and art pervades this novel and gives it its specific direction.

Creating images that expressed his state of mind became part of Emil Sinclair's "cure." In *Demian*, the omnipresent symbol of the hawk in the coat of arms of Sinclair's family is a striking example. "That night I dreamed about Demian and the coat of arms. It changed from one thing into another in a continual metamorphosis while Demian held it in his hands: now it was small and gray, now multicolored and tremendously large. He explained to me [Sinclair] that it nevertheless remained always one and the same. Finally he made me eat it. When I swallowed it, I felt, with monstrous horror, that the bird on the coat of arms I had swallowed was still alive inside me—it filled me entirely and started to eat away at me from the inside."[9] Awakening, Sinclair paints a picture of the heraldic bird that objectifies the mystery of the dream (70–71).

4

Levels of awareness, then, determine *Demian*'s meaning and design. Delving deeply into himself, Hesse created a form remarkable for its unique presentation of the individual within the "collective" unconscious *without* disturbing the interaction among characters expected of a conventional novel. Its dramatis personae are for the most part symbolic fictions, except for the narrator, Emil Sinclair, who stands out as the only fully developed character. For his story, Hesse used a time-honored German form of narrative, the so-called bildungsroman, a novel of education, which takes the reader from Sinclair's boyhood at the age of ten to his maturity at age twenty, roughly from 1906 to 1916.

We find that the world of his childhood is divided between "light" and "dark"—cleanliness and propriety set against dirt and fear, his own proper family against servants and laborers, criminals and people sick in hospitals. From then on, his education proceeds on two levels: daily life in a small town and a reality increasingly infused by "magic."

In order to impress an audience of village toughs (clearly inhabitants of the "dark" world), ten-year-old Sinclair falsely boasts that he has stolen a basket of apples. While Hesse probably had the first "forbidden fruit" in mind, he may have also thought of Saint Augustine's theft of a pear from a neighbor's tree in *Confessions*, Book 2. Franz Kromer, an older boy and leader of the toughs, blackmails Sinclair for a theft he had never committed, calling his victim by whistling. In European culture, the devil signals his presence or is summoned by a whistle, as illustrated in *Der Freischütz* by Carl Maria von Weber, which opera-loving Hesse probably knew, as well as in Boito's *Mefistofele*.

Under Kromer's diabolical extortions, Sinclair is reduced to stealing from his piggy bank, and he endures dreams that his tormentor is kneeling on top of him, forcing him to perform obscenities. In another nightmare he is even tricked into thinking of murdering his own father. The child's dream is rife with Freudian implications. Finally, Emil reaches a breaking point when his oppressor demands a meeting with one of his sisters.

Sinclair's education continues with his first rescue by a slightly older boy at school, Max Demian, the child/man with eyes "slightly sad, with flashes of mockery within them." Seeming to be an emissary from another world, Demian alleviates Sinclair's pain by the strength of his authority, which frightens Sinclair's tormentor. Neither an angel nor a minion of Satan but a guide in the spirit of Socrates' daemon, he leads Sinclair to ever greater heights of knowledge. This is, after all, a novel of education—for Hesse as well as his character. *Demian* may be seen as a "fiction of the self," presenting "a prophetic and highly didactic . . . version of the providential pattern of the Christian fall and redemption internalized in the narrator," as Eugene Stelzig puts it in his fine study called *Hermann Hesse's Fictions of the Self*.[10] Accordingly, the parables Hesse insists on early in the book revolve around Eden and its loss, exemplified by the idyllic side of small-town life shortly to be annihilated in the hellish chaos of war.

During this phase of his development, Sinclair gains a new kind of knowledge. Demian calls his attention to the emblem of the sparrow hawk above the door of the family house, which might once have been part of a monastery. This emblem, which the child had never stopped to think about, connects medieval symbolism to ancient Egyptian religions and therefore confers a mark of distinction on Sinclair's home.[11]

From this point on, each encounter has some symbolic or allegorical significance. The bildungsroman now assumes the nature of a quest. In an important essay titled "The Quest of the Grail in Hesse's *Demian*," Theodore Ziolkowski notes that the bildungsroman becomes a form of Perceval's quest for the Grail.[12] Even the most secularly inclined reader becomes aware of the religious nature of this pilgrimage into the deeper recesses of the self. The hero's descent into himself is a plunge into the supernatural and the divine. Demian, as Ziolkowski notes, "is a dictionary of religious lore."[13]

Another revelation concerns Demian's interpretation of the biblical account of Cain and Abel. In a letter written in 1930, Hesse identified Cain with Prometheus because he represents the intellect and freedom and was punished for his daring and inquiring mind.[14] This identification is already implied in his fiction of 1917–19, when Demian tells Sinclair that the Cain story was a slander invented by the weak to attack the strong.[15] Both the emblem of the sparrow hawk and Demian's version of the story of Cain are meant to indicate that Sinclair belongs to a chosen few, who will be recognizable by a mark on the forehead only they can see (20–25). In a similarly unorthodox way, Sinclair's mentor teaches that the thief on the cross to Christ's left was the worthier of the two condemned men. In an allusion to Friedrich Nietzsche's famous concept of the "transvaluation of values," exemplified in his book *Beyond Good and Evil* (1886),[16] Hesse here suggests that Demian, the daemon, is both infernal and divine.

5

With the onset of adolescence, the novel of education shifts to a new level. Sinclair attends secondary school in another town, where he rejects Demian's teaching and loses himself in heavy drinking and rowdy behavior. But, after a time, a change develops. Sinclair sees a lovely young girl and promptly falls in love with her. Although he never approaches her, he attempts to paint her portrait and calls her Beatrice. This is an allusion to Dante Gabriel Rossetti's painting *Beata Beatrix*, not to the woman who inspired Dante Alighieri, the poet of *The Divine*

Comedy. Sinclair's painting of the imaginary woman he loves, "an English pre-Raphaelite female figure, long-limbed and slender" with a "boyishness of form" (63), closely resembles Demian.[17] And like Rossetti's Beatrice, this ideal woman also leads Sinclair toward redemption.

This painting becomes the herald of a new vision. Home on vacation, Sinclair again meets Demian, who discerns in his friend's loose living a trace of Saint Augustine's portrayal of his earlier life in his *Confessions*, and is convinced that, like Augustine, Sinclair will rise above the herd to achieve a purified self (69). Demian's assessment is soon borne out. Back at school, under a dreamlike compulsion, Sinclair paints his heraldic hawk as it breaks out of its egg and sends the picture to his mentor. In reply, he receives a mysterious note from Demian: "The bird fights its way out of the egg. The egg is the world. Who ever wants to be born must destroy a world. The bird flies to god. The god is called Abraxas." The meaning of Abraxas is soon clarified for Sinclair in a lecture by a teacher as "something like a deity whose symbolic task is to unite the divine and the satanic" (75).

6

In the next stage of Sinclair's education, Demian is displaced by an eccentric organist named Pistorius, an interpreter of dreams and a familiar of Abraxas. Sinclair and Pistorius are soon bound by a close friendship. Pistorius is a thin disguise for Hesse's therapist and friend Dr. Josef Lang, whose favorite being was Abraxas. In fact, Hesse referred to Dr. Lang as Pistorius some years later in his semiautobiographical *Nuremberg Trip* (1927).[18]

Pistorius's lessons also include the importance of all religions as well as the belief that *the* reality, the *only* reality that counts, lies within. Here Hesse displayed the expertise he had gained from his analyst by putting into the words of Pistorius the recognition that Abraxas, a god also accepted and worshipped in gnosticism, is God and Satan in one. Although

Josef Lang was rooted in gnostic mysticism, a dualistic philosophy akin to Zoroastrianism that flowered during the early Christian era,[19] he gradually led Hesse beyond the implications of this system of beliefs.

Intellectually, as a growing young man, Hesse was deeply affected by two influential philosophers who were closely associated with Switzerland, his second home: Johann Jakob Bachofen, whose major work was on matriarchy and original religion, and, as noted before, Friedrich Nietzsche, whose state of mind served Hesse particularly well. Nietzsche's *Beyond Good and Evil* laid the foundation for Demian's teaching. Hesse similarly alluded to Nietzsche's *Thus Spoke Zarathustra* to convey a strong message that a powerful spirit can transcend the strife between good and evil.

Finally, Sinclair learns Demian's and Pistorius's lesson—that he must fear nothing. The soul's ideas are not to be exorcised or made the subject of moralizing. So-called temptations are to be treated with respect and love. All have meaning. In hating or loving someone, one hates or loves something in oneself. "The things we see," says Pistorius, "are the same things that are in us. There is no reality other than what we have inside us." At this point, having learned everything Pistorius has to teach, Sinclair breaks with his mentor, since each man must find the way to himself, "to feel your way forward along your own path, wherever it led."

After leaving Pistorius, Sinclair realizes that the demand for absolute concentration on the self has isolated him. It insulates him from anyone but a purified self, standing alone with "only the cold universe around you," like "Jesus in the Garden of Gethsemane." Inevitably, Sinclair's thinking draws him back to Demian until, finally, he writes a few words on a piece of paper. Though he intended to send this paper to Demian, he carries it with him instead and often recites the words to himself: "A guide has left me. I am in total darkness. I cannot take a single step alone. Help me!" (105).

7

The final stage of Sinclair's education is reached with the help of Demian's mother, Eve, alluded to throughout the novel. She is mentioned as the universal mother, a form of the Jungian "Earth Mother," magically linked to her magical son. In contrast to Sinclair's conventional family, no husband or father is ever mentioned in Demian's world. In fact, the mother/son connection is more like that of lovers, whose this-worldly bonds are incestuous. On the level of religious iconology, however, the bonds represent Eve, who not only signals the Fall but who is the universal mother of all humankind, as well as Mary—the New Eve—who with her son brings salvation.

A vision induced by Sinclair's growing awareness of his sexuality, from childhood to adulthood, pervades the entire novel and is made explicit in the final phase of the book. At the beginning of the chapter entitled "Eve," Hesse makes his point clear through a series of visual images. After an absence, Sinclair visits the house where Demian had once lived with his mother and sees an old woman in the garden. She takes him inside and shows him the photograph of a person who turns out to be Eve. His reaction is electrifying.

"[M]y heart stood still. — It was the picture from my dream! It was her: the large, almost masculine figure, resembling her son; the signs of maternal love, strictness, and deep passion in her features; beautiful and enticing, beautiful and unapproachable, daemon and mother, fate and lover. It was her!" The photo makes clear that "there was a woman . . . who bore the features of my destiny," and she had to be Demian's mother (106).

After Sinclair actually meets Eve in his and Demian's university town, a new phase begins. Slowly, the novel turns at last to the Great War, which had been a constant if covert theme, where Hesse suggests that the will of humanity "will reveal itself." It "stands written in individuals: in you and in me. It was there in Jesus, it was there in Nietzsche" (111).

Eve and her circle of friends and disciples echo these themes, and it soon becomes evident that mother and son represent a unity. They both bear the luminous Sign of Cain on their foreheads as do all those, including Sinclair, who share Demian's insights on the "herd" versus the individual. This mark, invisible to all except the initiates, distinguished the iconoclastic son of Adam. It appears on the few who are called to understand, accept, and represent Cain's defiance of conventional morality. The entire circle—but especially the "trinity" of Sinclair, Demian, and Eve—is united in a concentration of Nietzschean, Christian, and Eastern thought.

But there is a further bond. Emil Sinclair falls in love with Eve. "I stood there, deeply moved—I had so much joy and sorrow in my heart, as though everything I had ever done and ever felt was coming back to me in that moment, as answer, as fulfillment" (113). The same barely concealed passion that connects him to Demian now finds its true object in the mother with whom his daemon had been identified from the start. His place in their lives, their places in his own, are now clear where all the "seekers" who bear the Sign of Cain wait for a Messiah, while Europe is characterized as "an animal that has lain in chains for an eternity."

In Sinclair's unambiguously sexual feelings for Eve, Demian is at first included. However, Sinclair becomes depressed, waiting for "a great moment" when, as he hopes and expects, Eve will declare herself. He is tortured by desire. "I thought I could not bear seeing her next to me without taking her in my arms." But the wise woman he loves senses this at once and teaches restraint. "You mustn't have wishes you don't believe in. I know what you wish for" (120).

The plot of this deceptively simple tale shows that the surface narrative is "thin fare," as Joseph Mileck correctly observed in his discussion of *Demian*, but not so its underlying meaning.[20] At a later point, Sinclair dreams of climbing a tree or a tower and seeing an entire landscape ablaze. Eve has the same dream, and now at last their visions herald the outbreak of war. When Demian is called up as a lieutenant, he sends a final message to his friend and disciple, promising him that, if

he dies, he will come to him "in spirit and in truth," the words
of Christ. Demian reveals himself unmistakably as a savior-
figure.

8

Demian ends with a vision and its fulfillment. We now realize
that everything we read before was aimed at this defining moment. What we have seen up to now has been the chain of
memories the soldier Emil Sinclair—in love with Demian/
Eve—recalls as he stands guard in front of a Belgian farm. A
shell crashes near him.

> I could see a giant city in the clouds, with millions of people
> streaming out of it and swarming across the vast countryside. In
> their midst a powerful goddess-figure appeared, as large as a
> mountain range, with glittering stars in her hair and with Eve's
> features. The streams of people vanished into it as though into
> an enormous pit, and were gone. The goddess crouched on the
> ground and the mark on her brow glowed bright. She seemed in
> the grip of a dream: she closed her eyes, her huge face twisted in
> pain. Suddenly she shrieked, and stars leaped out of her brow,
> thousands of shining stars hurtling in magnificent arcs and
> semicircles across the black sky.

At that moment the soldier Sinclair also feels piercing pain
as the dream vision turns into reality. "One of these stars shot
straight at me with a shriek; it seemed to be trying to find
me. . . . Then it burst apart, screaming, into a thousand sparks,
flinging me up and then throwing me back to the ground. The
world collapsed in thunder above me" (134).

The dream vision takes place on several levels. The battlefield is torn by an exploding shell that "covers the entire
world." The goddess who reminds the soldier of Eve creates a
further dimension. We don't know yet whether the young soldier may lose Max Demian, his savior and mentor, through
death—a fate indicated by the exploding shell—or that he

himself may lie in the field hospital, badly wounded. We know only that this is war, that Sinclair is in combat, and there has just been a shattering explosion.

Told in the narrative past, this passage displays an overpowering dream vision: a million people stream out of a large city. We know it is a dream vision because it occurs in the clouds, and those millions of people are spread over an imaginary landscape. The godlike figure who assumes the features of Eve evokes, in turn, a vision from Revelation,[21] in which we are told of a woman clad in the sun, the moon beneath her feet, with a crown of twelve stars—a figure to be identified as the Virgin Mary—the New Eve.[22] But Hesse's new Eve does not give birth to the Christ child like the titanic figure in Revelation. Instead, "the ranks of the people were swallowed up into her as into a giant cave and vanished from sight." She cowers on the ground, cries out in pain, and from her forehead are born "many thousand shining stars," one of which contains the shrapnel that fells Sinclair.

The identity of Eve as the Primal Woman and as Mary, the Mother of God, creates a religious resolution to the struggle for meaning in a disastrous war: the ranks of the people that are swallowed up within Eve "as in a giant cave" represent the myriad war dead, and Eve becomes the Greek primal goddess Gaia, the Earth Mother who gives birth to all living things, and then, upon their deaths, receives them back into her "womb," the all-covering earth. Her cries of pain in Sinclair's vision represent her agony at receiving the dead, enough to fill a "huge city" with "millions of people."

The biblical allusions present pictorially and mythically Emil Sinclair's encounter with the tragedy of war. The brief passage that follows these images shows Sinclair finding himself on a hospital bed next to the dying Demian, who delivers his mother's saving kiss, merging the many layers of sexuality that pervade the book. On the physical level, homosexual impulses bind Sinclair to Demian; incestuous love binds Eve to both Sinclair and her son, Demian, in a deep threefold interconnection. But on a spiritual level, Hesse plumbs the depths of Christian symbolism and iconography. With her/his kiss,

Demian infuses the bleak panorama of war and death with spiritual hope. He tells Sinclair, "The next time you call me, I won't come so obviously on horseback or by train. You will have to listen inside yourself, and then you'll realize I'm in you" (135). Once again, he paraphrases the words of Jesus: "And behold, I am with you always, even unto the end of the world" (Matthew 28:20).

Hesse's words of 1962, the year of his death, provide a fitting conclusion to any consideration of *Demian* and the role of Sinclair in Hesse's life:

And beneath the sign of "Sinclair" there stands for me to this day that burning epoch, the dying of a beautiful and irretrievable world, that awakening, painful at first, then an intimately affirmative awakening to a new understanding of world and reality, the dazzling insight of unity within signs of polarity, the collapse of contraries into one another as the masters of Zen in China of millennia past had been able to put into magic formulae.[23]

Demian, a war novel in a deceptively simple, profoundly intricate form, contains Hesse's statement of a new faith in the self's inner truth, a truth beyond good and evil, and he couches it in a powerful synthesis of Christian and Eastern understanding of our world.

RALPH FREEDMAN

NOTES

1. "Introduction," Hermann Hesse, *Demian*, trans. Michael Roloff and Michael Lebeck (New York: Harper Collins, 1999), ix.
2. Even closer to our own time, *Demian* remained hugely attractive, selling as many as 1,486,000 copies in 1968 in the United States alone. See Rudolf Koester, "USA," in *Hermann Hesses weltweite Wirkung* (Hermann Hesse's Worldwide Effect), ed. Martin Pfeiffer (Frankfurt/Main: Suhrkamp Verlag, 1977), 163.

3. *Demian* (Roloff and Lebeck, 1999), 1. Further page references to this edition are noted in the text.

4. See Ralph Freedman, *Hermann Hesse: Pilgrim of Crisis* (New York: Pantheon Books, 1978), 192–93, henceforth cited as Freedman; and Joseph Mileck, *Hermann Hesse: Life and Art* (Berkeley: University of California Press, 1978), 88–89, henceforth cited as Mileck. A detailed account is rendered in German in *Materialien zu Hermann Hesses "Demian,"* ed. Volker Michels (Frankfurt/Main: Suhrkamp Verlag, 1993), 43.

5. See Mark Boulby, *Hermann Hesse: His Mind and Art* (Ithaca, NY: Cornell University Press, 1967), 82.

6 Freedman, 193; Mileck, 88.

7. Letter to Helene Welti in Hermann Hesse, *Gesammelte Briefe* I (May 18, 1916) (Frankfurt/Main: Suhrkamp Verlag, 2001) 324.

8. Hermann Hesse, *My Belief: Essays on Life and Art,* trans. Denver Lindley, ed. Theodore Ziolkowski (New York: Farrar, Straus & Giroux, 1974), 46–51. Emphasis mine.

9. The hawk or falcon has been used traditionally as a symbol of superiority or victory, since Horus, a falcon-headed ancient Egyptian deity, was the ultimate god of victory. Albrecht Dürer, in the engraving "The Arch of Triumph of Maximilian I," places a falcon on the terrestrial globe held in the emperor's left hand. Pietro de' Medici uses the symbol in a similar way in his coat of arms. See Guy de Tervarent, *Attributs et symbols dans l'art profance (1450–1600)* (Paris: Librairies Droz, 1958), s.v. *faucon.*

10. *Hermann Hesse's Fictions of the Self: Autobiography and the Confessional Imagination* (Princeton, NJ: Princeton University Press, 1965, 1988), 107.

11. Ibid.

12. Theodore Ziolkowski, "The Quest of the Grail in Hesse's *Demian,*" in *Hesse: A Collection of Critical Essays,* ed. Theodore Ziolkowski (Englewood Cliffs, NJ: Prentice Hall, 1973), 134–52.

13. "The Gospel of *Demian,*" in *The Novels of Hermann Hesse: A Study in Theme and Structure* (Princeton, NJ: Princeton University Press, 1965), 107.

14. Prometheus, an immortal Titan in Greek mythology, befriended mankind (and in some myths, created him). He stole fire from the gods and gave it to humans, teaching many arts and crafts. Zeus retaliated by chaining him to a mountain crag

and sending his eagle to devour his liver, an eternal torture. Prometheus has come to symbolize free-spirited revolt against authority.

15. In 1919, the year his novel was published, Hesse wrote a brief essay titled "Eigensinn" (Self-Will) that makes this point. *If the War Goes On*, trans. Ralph Manheim (New York: Farrar, Straus & Giroux, 1971), 79–85. Eugene Stelzig, in a brilliant chapter in *Hermann Hesse's Fictions of the Self*, shows how Hesse makes "self-will" into the theme that defines Sinclair and his "education" (43–79).

16. See Herbert W. Reichert, *The Impact of Nietzsche on Hermann Hesse* (Mt. Pleasant, MI: The Enigma Press), 40–42.

17. D(ante) G(abriel) Rossetti (1828–1882), originally named Gabriel Charles Dante, was a Victorian poet and painter who, because of his name, portrayed scenes from the great medievel poet Dante Alighieri's life, including portraits of the poet's beloved, Beatrice. The painting Hesse refers to, *Beata Beatrix*, is one of the most famous. For Hesse, however, the choice of Beatrice is no mere accident but a reference to the redeeming power of Dante's original beloved, now transferred to Emil Sinclair's mysterious young woman in the park. See also Stelzig, 146.

18. See, for example, Ralph Freedman, for a discussion in German of Dr. Lang's relation to Pistorius. "Abschied von allen Halbheiten" (Farewell to All Half-Measures), in *Kunst als Therapie. Hermann Hesse und die Psychoanalyse* (Art as Therapy: Hermann Hesse and Psychoanalysis), ed. Michael Limberg (Bad Liebenzell: Verlag Gengenbach, 1997), 97ff.

19. Zoroastrianism taught that salvation could only be attained through the occult knowledge (gnosis) revealed to the select. It taught that the world is ruled by *evil* forces, represented by the body and its desires. The God of the Old Testament holds the spirit of man captive, and Jesus was sent to restore knowledge of man's divine origin, leading to an upward struggle for the divine by suppressing the body as sin and filth.

20. Mileck, 98.

21. Chapter 12, verses 1–2.

22. See also Ziolkowski, *The Novels of Hermann Hesse*, 132.

23. "Vorwort zu Sinclairs Notizbuch" ("Foreword to Sinclair's Notebook"), new ed., 1962. See Hermann Hesse, *Gesammelte Werke* (Frankfurt/Main: Suhrkamp Verlag, 1970), 11–33. Translation mine.

Suggestions for Further Reading

Boulby, Mark. *Hermann Hesse: His Mind and Art*. Ithaca, NY: Cornell University Press, 1967. [*Demian*, 81–120.]

Casebeer, Edwin F. *Writers for the Seventies: Hermann Hesse*. New York: Warner, 1972. [Preface 19–22 passim. This interesting little book barely touches *Demian* but mentions the novel among a galaxy of works that define Hesse's reputation as part of the counterculture in America during the sixties.]

Cornils, Ingo. *A Companion to the Works of Hermann Hesse*. Rochester, NY: Camden House, 2009.

Cornils, Ingo. "From Outsider to Global Player: Hermann Hesse in the Twenty-First Century." In *A Companion to the Works of Hermann Hesse*, 1–16.

Crooke, William. *Mysticism and Modernity: Nationalism and the Irrational in Hermann Hesse, Robert Musil and Max Frisch*. Oxford: Peter Lang, 2008.

Field, George W. *Hermann Hesse*. New York: Twayne Publishers, 1970. [Chapter 4: "*Demian* and Symbols of Transformation," 41–61.]

Freedman, Ralph. *The Lyrical Novel: Studies in Hermann Hesse, André Gide, and Virginia Woolf*. Princeton, NJ: Princeton University Press, 1967. [*Demian*: "The Symbolic Hero," 57–71.]

———. *Hermann Hesse: Pilgrim of Crisis*. New York: Pantheon Books, 1978. [Chapter 5: "From Crisis to War," *Demian*, including Hesse's breakdown and cure by Dr. Lang, 183–93.]

Gullatz, Stefan. "*Demian* and the Lacanian Gaze." In Ingo Cornils, ed., *Hermann Hesse Today*, 173–85. Amsterdam, Netherlands: Rodopi, 2005.

Michels, Volker. "Hermann Hesse and Psychoanalysis." In Ingo Cornils, *A Companion to the Works of Hermann Hesse*, 323–44.

Mileck, Joseph. *Hermann Hesse: Life and Art*. Berkeley: University of California Press, 1978. [*Demian*: Emancipation and Quest,

Sigmund Freud and Carl Gustav Jung, Psychoanalysis and Literature, 88–108.]

Robertson, Ritchie. "Gender Anxiety and the Shaping of the Self in Some Modernist Writers (Musil, Hesse, Hofmannsthal, Jahnn)." In Graham Bartram, ed., *The Cambridge Companion to the Modern German Novel*, 46–61. Cambridge: Cambridge University Press, 2004.

Rose, Ernst. *Faith from the Abyss: Hermann Hesse's Way from Romanticism to Modernity*. London: Peter Owen, 1965. ["The End of an Era: Psychoanalysis and *Demian*," 47–56.]

Seidlin, Oskar. "Hermann Hesse: The Exorcism of the Demon." In Ziolkowski, *Hesse: A Collection of Critical Essays*, 51–75.

Solbach, Andras, "The Aesthetics of Ritual: Pollution, Magi, and Sentimentality in Hesse's *Demian* (1919)" In Ingo Cornils, *A Companion to the Works of Hermann Hesse*, 81–115.

Stelzig, Eugene L. *Hermann Hesse's Fictions of the Self: Autobiography and the Confessional Imagination*. Princeton, NJ: Princeton University Press, 1988. [This book includes many important references to *Demian*. They are coherently presented in "*Demian* and the Decline of Europe," 150–54.]

Tusken, Lewis W. *Hermann Hesse: The Man, His Myth, His Metaphor*. Columbia: University of South Carolina Press, 1998. [*Demian*: Chapter 7: "*Demian's Rebirth*," 84–97.]

Wilson, Colin. *Hermann Hesse*. New York: Village Press, 1974. [*Demian*, 29–31. Brief comments by the author of *The Outsider* who first described Hesse as a leader of the counterculture during the fifties.]

Ziolkowski, Theodore. *The Novels of Hermann Hesse: A Study in Theme and Structure*. Princeton, NJ: Princeton University Press, 1965. [Chapter 7: "The Gospel of *Demian*," 87–145.]

———. *Fictional Representations of Jesus*. Princeton, NJ: Princeton University Press, 1972. [The figure of Demian is one of these representations.]

———, ed. *Hesse: A Collection of Critical Essays*. Englewood Cliffs, NJ: Prentice Hall, 1973.

———. "The Quest for the Grail." In Ziolkowski, *Hesse: A Collection of Critical Essays*, 134–52.

RECOMMENDED COLLECTIONS OF
HESSE'S ESSAYS

If the War Goes On. Trans. Ralph Manheim. New York: Farrar, Straus & Giroux, 1971. [Includes Hesse's essay, "Self-Will" (1919).]

Autobiographical Writings. Trans. Denver Lindley. New York: Farrar, Straus & Giroux, 1972.

My Belief: Essays on Life and Art. Trans. Denver Lindley. Ed. Theodore Ziolkowski. New York: Farrar, Straus & Giroux, 1974. [Includes Hesse's essay "Artists and Psychoanalysis," 1918.]

Reflections. Trans. Ralph Manheim. New York: Farrar, Straus & Giroux, 1974.

All I wanted to do was try to live the life that was inside me, trying to get out. Why was that so hard?

Demian

To tell my story, I have to start very far back. In fact, if I could, I would have to go back much farther—to the very first years of my childhood, or even farther back, into the distant reaches of my origins.

When writers write novels, they tend to act as though they were God, who can see and understand anything and everything about a person's story, and they present that story as though God himself were telling it, without all the veils of disguise that are the fundamental nature of life. I cannot do that—any more than these writers can. But my story is more important to me than some writer's story is to him, because it is my own, and it is the story of a human being—not an imagined, possible, ideal, or in some other way nonexistent person but a real, unique, living, breathing one. Now we know much less today than ever before about what that is—a real living person—and as a result, people, each of them a precious, unique creation of nature, are being shot dead in enormous numbers. If each one of us were no more than a single human being, if the world really could completely be rid of us with a single bullet, then there would be no sense in telling stories anymore. But every person is more than himself: he is also the unique, entirely particular, and in every case meaningful and remarkable point of intersection where the phenomena of the world overlap, only once and never again in just this way. That is why everyone's story is important, eternal, and godlike— why everyone, as long as and in whatever fashion he lives and fulfills the will of Nature, is wonderful and worthy of all our attention. Everyone is the spirit made flesh; in everyone, creation takes form and suffers; in everyone, a Redeemer dies on the cross.

Few know what a person is these days. But many feel it, and can die more easily, the way I will die more easily once I have written out this story to the end.

I cannot claim to possess any knowledge. I was a seeker, and I still am. But I no longer look to the stars, or seek in books; I have started to hear the lessons roared and murmured by the blood in my body. My story is not a happy one, not pleasing and harmonious like something invented—it reeks of meaninglessness and confusion, of insanity and dream, like the life of anyone who no longer wants to lie to himself.

Everyone's life is a way into himself, or the attempt at a way, the hint of a path. No one is utterly and completely himself; everyone strives to become himself, however he can, this one dully, that one more brightly. We all carry traces of our birth with us to the end—the slime and eggshell of a primeval past. Some of us never become human, but stay a frog, a lizard, an ant. Some are human from the waist up and fish from the waist down. But everyone is a stab at humanity, a roll of Nature's dice. We all share a common origin, our mothers; we all come out of the same gaping maw; but every one of us struggles—an attempt, a throw from the depths—to reach our own individual goal. We can understand each other, but each of us can truly grasp and interpret only himself.

CHAPTER ONE

TWO WORLDS

I will begin my story with something that happened to me when I was ten years old and going to the Latin school in our small town.

All sorts of sights and smells come back to me, rise up from within me, to touch me with an ache and a blissful shudder—dark streets and bright streets, houses and towers, clocks striking the hour, people's faces, rooms full of warm and homey comforts, rooms full of secrets and of a deep fear of ghosts. There is the scent of warm, close spaces, of rabbits and serving girls, of household remedies and dried fruit. Two worlds intermingled there; from two opposite poles came the day and the night.

One world was the parental home, but actually it was even narrower—in truth it contained only my parents. On the whole I knew this world well: its name was Mother and Father, it was love and strict rules, education and example. What belonged to this world was gently shining radiance, clarity, and cleanliness; quiet, friendly conversation; washed hands, clean clothes, good behavior. Morning hymns were sung there, Christmas celebrated. In that world of straight lines and paths leading into the future, there was duty and obligation, bad conscience and confessions, forgiveness and good resolutions, love and respect, wisdom and Biblical proverbs. You had to keep to this world for your life to be clear and pure, beautiful and harmonious.

Meanwhile the other world was there already, right in the middle of our house and completely different: it smelled different, spoke differently, promised and demanded entirely different things. There were serving girls and traveling tradesmen in this second world, ghost stories and scandalous rumors, a richly colored flood of monstrous, tempting, frightening, mysterious things like the slaughterhouse and the prison, alcoholics and bickering women, cows giving birth and horses with broken legs, and stories of burglaries, murders, suicides. All these beautiful, horrible, wild, cruel things existed all around—in the next street over, in the house next door. Policemen and beggars ran around, drunks beat their wives, gaggles of girls poured out of the factories after work, old women could cast a spell on you and make you sick, bands of robbers were living in the forest, arsonists were being caught by the country police—this powerful second world welled up everywhere, its scent was everywhere, except in our rooms where Mother and Father were. And that was good. How wonderful that here, in our home, there was peace and calm and order, duty and conscience, mercy and love—and how wonderful that all the rest existed too, everything loud and shrill, dark and violent, from which you could still escape to Mother in a single bound.

The strangest thing was how these two worlds touched each other, how close to each other they were! For example, our maid Lina, when she sat with her freshly washed hands resting on the apron she had smoothed down on her lap, praying by the door of our living room and joining her bright voice to our song, belonged completely to Mother and Father, to we who lived in the world of light and truth. The next moment, in the kitchen or the barn, when she told me the story of the little man with no head, or fought with the neighbor women at the butcher shop, she was someone else and a part of the other world, and was shrouded in mystery. That's how it was with everyone, most of all myself. Of course I was part of the bright and true world—I was my parents' child—but wherever I turned my eye or ear the other world was always there, and I lived in the other world too, even though it often felt like I didn't belong there, in the spooky realm of fear and bad conscience. At times I even liked the forbidden world best, and often my return to the light, as good and necessary as it might be, felt almost like a turn toward something less beautiful, less exciting, more desolate and dreary. Sometimes I knew that my goal in life was to turn into someone like my father and my mother: so bright and pure, so superior and harmonious. But it was a long, long way to that goal, and along that way you had to sit quietly in school and study and take tests and pass exams, and all the while the path ran right past the other, darker world, or through it, and it was by no means impossible to stay in it, drown in it. There were stories of the lost boys, prodigal sons, that this had happened to, and I read them avidly. The return to the father, to what was good, was always such a magnificent liberation in these stories—I was perfectly aware that this was the only right and good and desirable outcome; but still, the part of the story that took place among the lost and evil souls was always much more exciting, and, if it were only possible to admit it, it was sometimes actually rather a shame that the lost soul had to repent and be found again. But that was something you didn't say, and didn't even think. It was just there, somehow, as a hunch or a possibility buried deep, deep down in your feelings. When I imagined the devil, I could see him perfectly well on the street down the hill, in disguise or not, or at the fair, or in a pub—but never with us at home.

My sisters were also part of the brightly lit world. I often felt they were naturally more like Father and Mother than I was—more well-behaved, more perfect, better. They had their faults, and bad habits, but ones that never ran very deep, I felt. Not like with me, where any contact with evil was so painful and difficult, and where the dark world seemed to lie so much closer. Sisters, like parents, were there to take care of and respect, and whenever you fought with them it was always you that your conscience said was the bad one, the cause of the problem, the one who had to ask for forgiveness, because to offend your sisters was to offend your parents, the benevolent authority figures. There were secrets I could share with the worst delinquents from the street much more readily than with my sisters. On good days, when the air was bright and my conscience was clear, I was often delighted to play with my sisters, to behave well with them and see myself in a good, noble light.

That was what life must be like as an angel! That was the highest state we could imagine, and we thought how sweet and wonderful it would be to be angels, wrapped in a bright clear sound and smell like Christmas and happiness. But oh, how rare such good days were! Many times, even when playing a harmless, permitted game, I played with too much passion and force for my sisters, which led to accidents, or fights, and then, when anger and rage came over me, I was horrible and said and did things whose depravity I could feel, deep and burning, even while I was doing and saying them. Then came dark and bitter hours of regret and remorse, and then the painful moment when I asked for forgiveness, and then again a beam of bright light—quiet, grateful, harmonious happiness for a few more hours, or minutes.

I was a student in the Latin school, with the mayor's son and head forester's son in my class. They would come over to my house sometimes; they were wild boys, yet they belonged to the good, unforbidden world. But I also did things with neighborhood boys from the public school, boys we otherwise looked down on. It is with one of them that my story begins.

One afternoon that we had off from school—I was a little over ten years old—I was exploring with two boys from the neighborhood. Then a bigger kid came up to us, a tailor's son, rowdy and strong, thirteen years old, from the public school. His father was a drinker and the whole family had a bad reputation. I knew a lot about him, this Franz Kromer; I was afraid of him, and I was not happy that he was joining us. He already affected the behavior of a grown man, imitating how the factory workers walked and talked. We followed his lead and climbed down to the riverbank next to the bridge, hiding away from the world under the first arch. The narrow strip of shore between the bridge's bulging wall and the sluggishly flowing river was covered with nothing but garbage, rubble, and junk—tangled heaps of rusted steel wire and the like. Every so often you could find something usable there; Franz Kromer made us search with him and show him whatever we found. Then he would either put it in his pocket or throw it far out into the river. He told us to keep an eye out for anything made of lead, brass, or tin, which he always kept; he pocketed an old ivory comb too. I felt uneasy around him, not because I knew that my father would have forbidden what we were doing, but because I was afraid of Franz himself. Still, I was glad he accepted me and treated me like the others. He ordered and we obeyed, as though out of long-standing custom, even though this was the first time I was with him.

Eventually, we sat down on the ground. Franz spat into the water, looking like a man; he spat between a gap in his teeth and could hit anything he wanted. A conversation started, and the boys started bragging and complimenting themselves on all kinds of schoolboy heroics and pranks they had pulled off. I kept quiet, but I was afraid I would stand out for just that reason and draw Kromer's anger. My two companions had gone over to his side from the start and kept their distance from me; I was the outsider, and I felt that my clothes and my whole way of acting was a kind of challenge to them. As a student at the Latin school and the son of a well-to-do father, there was no way Franz could possibly like me, and I felt sure that the other two would abandon me without a second thought, if it ever came to that.

Finally, out of sheer fear, I began to talk too. I made up a grand story about robbers, with myself as the hero. One night, I said, in an orchard by the corner mill, I had stolen a whole sack of apples with a friend, and no ordinary apples either, but the best kinds, Reine de Reinettes and Golden Pearmains. I sought refuge from my dangerous situation in this story; making up and telling stories came quickly and easily to me. Then, so I wouldn't have to stop so soon and possibly end up in an even worse predicament, I gave my talent full rein: One of us, I said, had had to keep watch the whole time while the other was in the tree tossing down the apples, and in the end the sack had gotten so heavy that we had to leave half the apples behind, but half an hour later we came back for the rest.

When I was done I expected them to show their approval. I had warmed up by the end and was intoxicated with my own imagination. The two younger boys said nothing, waiting to see how Franz Kromer reacted, while he just gave me a pene-

trating look with half-squinting eyes then asked me in a threatening voice: "Is that true?"

"Of course," I said.

"Really and truly?"

"Yes, really and truly," I insisted, while on the inside I was
choking with fear.

"Would you swear to it?"

I was terrified, but I instantly said Yes.

"Say: By God and everything holy."

I said: "By God and everything holy."

"All right then," he said, and he turned away.

I thought everything had turned out all right, and I was glad
when, before long, he stood up and started back. When we
were on the bridge I said timidly that I had to go home now.

"There's no hurry," Fritz said with a laugh. "We're going
the same way."

He slowly strolled on, and I didn't dare to run off, but he really was walking the way to our house. When we got there,
when I saw our front door and its thick brass handle, the sun
in the windows and the curtains in my mother's room, I
breathed a deep sigh. Back home! Oh, the good, the blessed
return to our house, to brightness and peace!

I quickly opened the door and slipped inside and was about
to shut the door behind me when Franz Kromer pushed his
way in. In the cool, dim, tiled hallway, with no light except
what came in from the courtyard, he stood in front of me,
grabbed my arm, and said softly: "Not so fast, you!"

I looked at him, frightened. His grip on my arm was like
iron. I tried to imagine what he might have in mind, whether
he wanted to hurt me. If I screamed now, I thought, a loud
strong scream, would someone from up there get down here
quickly enough to save me? But I didn't do it.

"What?" I asked. "What do you want?"

"Nothing much. I just need to ask you something. The others don't need to hear it."

"Well? What do you want me to tell you? I have to go upstairs, you know."

"You do know who the fruit orchard next to the mill belongs to, don't you?" Franz said quietly.

"No, I don't know. The miller, I think."

Franz had put his arm around me, and he pulled me right up to his face so that I had to look into it from close up. His eyes were evil, he smiled a nasty smile, and his face was full of cruelty and power.

"Well, my boy, I can tell you whose orchard it is. I've known for a long time that someone had stolen his apples, and I also know that he said he would give two marks to anyone who told him who'd taken them."

"My God!" I cried. "You won't tell him, will you?"

I could see there was no point appealing to his sense of honor. He was from the other world: for him, betrayal was not a crime. I felt this perfectly clearly. In such matters, people from the "other" world were not like us.

"Not tell him?" Kromer laughed. "Who do you think I am, my friend, some kind of counterfeiter who can make a two-mark coin for myself? I'm poor. I don't have a rich father like you. If I can get two marks I have to do it. Maybe he'll even give me more."

He suddenly let go of me. Our front hall no longer smelled of peace and security—the world was collapsing around me. He would report me, I was a criminal, they would tell my father, maybe even the police would come. All the terrors of chaos threatened me; everything ugly and dangerous had been called up against me. The fact that I hadn't actually stolen any apples meant absolutely nothing—I had sworn the opposite. My God, my God!

Tears came to my eyes. I felt I had to buy my way free, and I desperately searched through my pockets. No apple, no pocket knife—nothing there. Then I thought of my watch. It was an old silver watch that didn't work; I wore it "just because." It had been our grandmother's. I quickly pulled it out of my pocket.

"Kromer, listen," I said, "you can't turn me in, that wouldn't be right. I'll give you my watch here, look, I'm sorry but I don't have anything else. You can have it, it's made of silver, the works are good, there's just a little something wrong with it, it needs to be fixed."

He smiled and took the watch in his large hand. I looked at that hand and could feel how savage and deeply hostile to me it was, how it was reaching out for my life and my peace.

"It's silver. . . ." I said timidly.

"What do I care about your silver or your old watch!" he said contemptuously. "Go fix it yourself!"

"But Franz," I cried, trembling with fear that he might run off. "Wait a minute! Take the watch! It's really made of silver, really and truly. And I don't have anything else."

He looked at me coolly, scornfully.

"Well then, you know who I'm going to have to pay a visit to. Or I could tell the police, I know the sergeant."

He turned to go. I held him back by the sleeve. He couldn't! I would rather die than face everything that would happen if he left like that.

"Franz!" I begged, my voice hoarse. "Don't do anything silly! You're just playing, right?"

"Sure, I'm playing, but this game might get expensive for you."

"Tell me what I can do, Franz! I'll do anything!"

He sized me up with his squinty eyes and laughed again.

"Don't be so stupid!" he said in a fake-cheery voice. "You know as well as I do. I could get two marks for telling, and I'm not a rich man, I can't just throw away two marks. You know that. But you're rich, you even have a watch. So you just need to give me the two marks, then everything will be fine."

I could understand the logic, but two marks! That was as unattainable for me as ten, or a hundred, or a thousand. I didn't have any money. There was a piggy bank that my mother kept, with a couple five- or ten-cent coins inside from visiting uncles. Other than that I had nothing. I had not started to get an allowance at that age.

"I don't have anything," I said sadly. "No money at all. I'll give you everything else I have. A cowboy and Indian book, and soldiers, and a compass—I'll go get them."

Kromer just sneered with his arrogant, wicked mouth and spat on the floor.

"Enough with your babbling!" he ordered. "You can keep your junk. A compass! Don't make me mad, you hear? I want the money!"

"But I don't have any, I never get any money. There's nothing I can do about it!"

"Well tomorrow you'll bring me the two marks. I'll wait for you after school down by the market. Period. If you don't bring the money, you'll see what happens!"

"Yes, but, where can I get it? Good God, if I don't have any—"

"That's your problem. There's money in your house. So, tomorrow after school. And I'm telling you, if you don't have it. . . ." He looked me in the eye with a terrible look, spat one more time, and was gone like a shadow.

I could not go upstairs. My life was ruined. I thought about running away and never coming back, or drowning myself, but only vaguely. I sat down in the dark on the bottom step of our stairway, crawled deep inside myself, and gave myself over to my misery. Lina found me crying there when she came downstairs with the basket to fetch wood.

I asked her not to say anything to the others and went upstairs. On the rack next to the glass doors hung my father's hat and my mother's parasol—domestic tenderness streamed forth from these things and my heart went out to them, pleading and grateful, like the prodigal son when he first saw and smelled his old rooms back home. But none of it was mine anymore, it was all the clear, bright Father-and-Mother-world while I had sunk deeply and guiltily into the other flood, tangled in sin and adventure and threatened by enemies, with no hope of anything but danger, fear, and shame. The hat and the parasol, the good old sandstone floor, the large picture above the hall closet, the voice of my older sister coming from the living room—they were all dearer, all more precious and delicate than ever, but no longer any consolation or safely in my possession, just accusations and reproaches. None of it was mine anymore—I no longer had any part in its quiet good cheer. I had dirt on my feet that I couldn't scrape off on the mat; I carried with me a shadow that the world of home knew nothing about. I had already had so many secrets, been so often scared, but compared to what I had brought home with me today, those were all just fun and games. Now destiny was pursuing me; hands were reaching out for me that my mother could not protect me from, she must never even find out about them. Whether my crime was stealing or lying (had I not sworn a false oath by God and everything holy?)—that made no difference. My sin was not this or that in particular, my sin was that I had reached out my hand to the devil. Why had I gone with him? Why had I listened to Kromer more obediently than I did to my father? Why had I lied and made up that story about stealing the apples? Boasted about a crime as though it were a great accomplishment? Now I was hand in hand with the devil; now the enemy was right behind me.

For a moment I wasn't afraid of what would happen tomorrow, but mainly of the terrible certain truth that my path now led farther and farther down into darkness. I could sense with perfect clarity that my misdeed would necessarily give rise to new misdeeds, and that showing my face to my sisters, hugging and kissing my parents, would now be a lie—I now carried within me a destiny and a secret that I had to keep hidden.

I felt a burst of hope and trust for a moment when I saw my father's hat. I would tell him everything, accept his judgment and his punishment, and make him my confessor and savior. It would just be a penance like the many I had been through before—a hard, bitter hour and a hard, regretful plea for forgiveness.

How sweet that sounded! How beautiful and tempting it was! But it was no use. I knew I wouldn't do it. I knew I now had a secret, a guilt, that I had to expiate alone. Maybe this was the very moment I was at the crossroads: maybe it was from now on that I would belong on the side of the bad, for ever and ever, share secrets with evil people, depend on them, obey them, and have no choice but to be one of them. I had pretended to be a man and a hero, and now I had to bear the consequences.

I was glad my father was angry about my wet shoes when I walked in the room. It was a distraction; he didn't notice anything worse, and it was easy enough to accept a criticism that I secretly transferred onto other offenses. With this, the flicker of a strange new feeling rose up within me, wicked, barbed, and stinging: I felt superior to my father! I felt, for a moment, a kind of contempt for his ignorance of the truth, and his scolding me about my wet shoes seemed petty. "If you only knew!" I thought, and I felt like a criminal being questioned about a stolen bread roll when actually he had committed a murder. It was an ugly, repellent feeling, but it was strong, and there was something deeply exciting about it. And it created a tighter bond between myself and my guilty secret than anything else had. Maybe Kromer has already gone to the police and reported me, I thought, maybe the storm clouds are already gathering over my head while here they're treating me like a little child!

That moment was the most important one of the whole experience thus far, with the most lasting effects. The sacred inviolability of my father was torn for the first time; it was the first crack in the pillars on which my young life rested and which everyone has to pull down before he can become himself. The essential inner line of our destiny consists of these invisible experiences. Such cracks and tears heal, they grow back together and are forgotten, but down in our most secret recesses, they continue to live and bleed.

I was immediately terrified of this new feeling. I wanted to throw myself at my father's feet at once and kiss them, beg his pardon. But there is no way to apologize for anything truly fundamental, and a child feels this and knows it as deeply and inwardly as any wise man.

I felt a need to think about my situation and come up with a course of action for the next day. But I couldn't do it. All I did that whole evening was slowly get used to the changed atmosphere of our living room. The clock on the wall, the table, the

Bible and the mirror, the bookshelf and the pictures on the wall—they all bade me farewell; I had to look on, my heart growing cold within me, as my world—my beloved, happy life—detached itself from me and turned into the past. I could not help but feel myself putting down roots that from now on would hold me fast in the foreign land of darkness outside. For the first time I tasted death, and death tastes bitter because it is birth: anxiety and terror in the face of frightening renewal.

How happy I was to finally lie down in my bed again! Beforehand, as one last purgatory, came evening prayers, and the hymn we sang that night was one of my favorites. But no, I did not sing along—every note was gall and wormwood for me. When my father spoke the blessing I did not pray with the others, and when he ended with " . . . be with us all!" a kind of convulsion ripped me out of the family circle. The grace of God was with them all, but no longer with me. I left the room feeling cold and deeply exhausted.

In bed, after I had lain there a while tenderly wrapped in warmth and comfort, my heart once again strayed back to my fear, fluttering anxiously around what had happened. My mother had said goodnight to me as always; her footsteps still echoed in the room, and the glow from her candle still shone in the crack beneath the door. Now, I thought, she'll come back now—she has felt something, she will give me a kiss and ask me about it, full of love and forgiveness, and I'll be able to cry, the lump in my throat will melt away, and I'll hug her and tell her and everything will be good again, then I'll be saved! When the crack beneath the door grew dark again, I listened for a while longer and thought that it had to happen, it had to.

Then I returned to the situation at hand and faced my enemy straight on. I could see him clearly: he had a squinty eye, his mouth was mocking me with a rough laugh, and while I looked at him and a sense of inescapable fate gnawed away at me, he grew bigger and uglier, and his evil eye flashed like the devil's. He was right next to me until I fell asleep, but then I did not dream about him or anything that had happened that day. Instead I dreamed we were sailing in a boat, my parents and sisters and me, surrounded by the peace and radiance of a holiday. I woke up in the middle of the night and could still feel the aftertaste of that blessedness—could still see my sisters' white summer dresses shimmering in the sun—and I fell from that paradise back into what was. Again I was standing face to face with the enemy and his evil eye.

The next morning, when my mother hurried into the room, yelling that it was late and why was I still lying in bed, I looked sick, and when she asked me if something was wrong, I threw up.

That seemed to be a victory of sorts. I always loved it when I was a little sick and could spend the whole morning lying in bed with a cup of chamomile tea, listening to Mother straightening up in the next room and Lina talking to the butcher out in the front hall. A morning home from school had something magical about it, like a fairy tale; the sun would come playfully into the room, and it was not the same sun as the one the green shades in the schoolroom were pulled down to block. But today even this felt off, struck a wrong note.

Yes, if only I died! But I was just a little sick, as I had been many times before; none of my problems had been solved. Being sick kept me out of school but in no way kept me from Kromer, who would be waiting for me in the market square at eleven o'clock. Mother's kindness did not console me this time either: it was a painful burden. I quickly pretended to fall back asleep and thought about what to do. Nothing made any difference—I had to be at the market square at eleven. So I quietly got up at ten and said I was feeling better. As usual, Mother told me I had to either go back to bed or go to school for the afternoon. I said I wanted to go to school. I had come up with a plan.

I couldn't meet Kromer without any money at all. I had to get the little stash that belonged to me. There was not enough money in the box, I knew that, but at least there was something, and I had a sense that anything would be better than nothing—Kromer had to be placated in some way.

I felt bad when I crept into Mother's room in my socks and took the money box out of her desk, but not as bad as I had felt the day before. The pounding of my heart made me feel like I was about to throw up again, and it was no better when I realized, at the bottom of stairs, that the box was locked. It was easy to break it open—there was only a thin tin grate to tear off—but it hurt to break it: only then, by doing that, had I committed robbery. Before that I had snuck a treat here and there, candy or fruit, but this was theft, even if it was my own money. I felt I had now taken another step closer to Kromer and his world, and how quick and easy it was to go downward, step by step. I suddenly felt defiant: Let the devil take me! There's no turning back now. I nervously counted out the money—the box had sounded so full, but now, in my hand, there was so pathetically little. Sixty-five cents. I hid the box in the downstairs hallway, held the money in my fist, and left the house, differently from every other time I had gone out the front gate. Upstairs I thought I heard someone calling after me; I ran away.

There was still a lot of time. I took a long way, full of detours, slipping through the streets of a changed city under clouds I had never seen before, past houses that were looking at me, people who were suspicious of me. I suddenly remembered that a school friend of mine had once found a thaler coin at the cattle market; I wanted to pray for a miracle from God, that He would let me make such a find, but I knew I no longer had any right to pray. And even if I had found the money, my money box would still be broken.

Franz Kromer saw me from a distance but came up slowly, not seeming to pay any attention to me. When he was close he made a gesture ordering me to follow him and walked on calmly, without turning around even once, down Strohgasse and across the footbridge to a construction site at the edge of town. No one was working there; the walls were bare, without doors or windows in the frames yet. Kromer looked around and then stepped through an empty doorway. I followed him. He walked behind a wall, waved me over, and stretched out his hand.

"D'you have it?" he asked coolly.

I pulled my clenched hand out of my pocket and shook the

money into his palm. He had counted it even before the last five-cent piece had stopped clinking.

"That's sixty-five cents," he said, and he looked at me.

"Yes," I said timidly. "That's all I have. I know it's too little, but it's everything. I don't have any more."

"I thought you were smarter than that," he scolded me almost gently. "Men of honor do things the right way. I'm not going to let you give me anything that isn't the right amount, you know that. Here, keep your nickels! The other guy—you know who I mean—he won't try to knock down the price. He'll pay."

"But I don't have any more! That was everything in my money box!"

"That's your business. But I don't want to make you unhappy. You still owe me one mark and thirty-five cents. When am I gonna get it?"

"Oh, you'll get it, Kromer, definitely! I don't know right now—maybe I'll get more soon, tomorrow or the day after. I can't tell my father, you understand."

"I don't care about that. I'm not the kind of person who wants to hurt you. I could have my money before lunchtime, you know, and I'm poor. You have nice clothes on, you get better food to eat for lunch than I do, but I won't say anything. I'll wait a little while. The day after tomorrow I'll whistle for you, in the afternoon, and you can take care of it then. You know my whistle?"

He whistled for me. I had heard it many times before.

"Yes," I said, "I know it."

He walked off as though we didn't know each other. It was just business between us, nothing more.

I think if I suddenly heard Kromer's whistle again, even now, so many years later, it would scare me. From that day on I heard it often—it felt like I heard it constantly. There was no place, no game, no task, no thought that his whistle didn't force its way into, robbing me of my independence. That whistle was now my destiny. Many a time, on mild and colorful autumn afternoons, I would be in our little flower garden, which I loved, and a strange urge would make me return to the boy's games of an earlier time in my life: I was acting the part, you might say, of a younger boy, still good and free, sheltered and innocent. But then Kromer's whistle, never entirely unexpected but still always a terrible shock, would come bursting in from somewhere or other, to cut the threads, destroy the games I was imagining. Then I had to go and follow my tormentor to nasty, ugly places, give him a full report, and listen to him warn me to hurry up with the money. The whole thing lasted maybe a few weeks, but to me it seemed like years, an eternity. I almost never had money to give him, at most a five- or ten-cent piece I had stolen from the kitchen table when Lina had left it there. Every time, Kromer berated and cursed me, showering me with contempt: *I* was the one betraying *him,* keeping from him what was rightfully his; I was the one robbing him, making him unhappy! Rarely in my life have I suffered so deeply, and never have I felt greater hopelessness, greater dependence.

I had refilled the money box with toy coins and put it back; no one asked about it. But that could come crashing down on my head at any moment too. There were many times I was even more afraid of my mother's soft footsteps than of Kromer's brutal whistle—might she not be coming to ask about the money box?

When I had showed up too many times without money for my devil, he started to torture and use me in other ways. I had to work for him. He had to deliver packages for his father, so I had to deliver packages for him. Or else he gave me a difficult task to do, like hop on one leg for ten minutes straight or stick a note on a passerby's jacket. I would continue and multiply these torments myself, in nightmares, lying in a pool of sweat.

For a while it made me sick. I threw up often, had chills by day and sweats and fevers by night. My mother could tell something was wrong and took tender care of me, which only made it worse, since I couldn't trust and confide in her in return.

One night, after I'd gone to bed, she brought me a little piece of chocolate. It was an echo of years past, when I would often get a comforting little treat at night when I had been good. This time, when she stood there and held out a piece of chocolate for me, I was so sore of heart that I could only shake my head. She asked what was wrong and stroked my hair. I could only blurt out: "No! No! I don't want anything." She put the chocolate down on the nightstand and left. The next day, when she tried to ask me about what had happened, I pretended not to know what she meant. Another time she took me to the doctor; he examined me and prescribed washing in cold water every morning.

My condition during that period was like a kind of insanity. In the middle of the well-ordered, harmonious peace of our house, I lived shy and tormented like a ghost; I did not share in the others' lives and could rarely forget my situation for even an hour. My father was often annoyed, and whenever he confronted me I was cold and reserved back.

CHAPTER TWO

CAIN

Salvation from my torments came from an entirely unexpected direction, and along with salvation something new came into my life whose effects have continued to this day.

A new student had recently appeared in our Latin school. He was the son of a well-to-do widow who had moved to our city; he wore a black ribbon of mourning on his sleeve. He entered a higher grade than mine and was several years older than me, but before long I noticed him, just as everyone else did. This remarkable student seemed to be much older than he looked—he didn't come across as a schoolboy to anyone. He moved like a man among us children, a man from a different world—actually, like a lord. He was not liked; he never took part in our games, much less any rough-housing. The only thing anyone liked about him was the firm and confident tone he took with the teacher. His name was Max Demian.

One day, as sometimes happened in our school for whatever reason, a different grade had classes in our own grade's large schoolroom. It was Demian's class. We younger students had Bible class that day; the older students had to write an essay. While the teacher drummed the story of Cain and Abel into our heads, I kept looking over at Demian, whose face strangely fascinated me: I saw his bright, unusually determined and intelligent face bent attentively over his work, looking nothing at all like a student doing an assignment, but rather like a scholar or scientist conducting his own research. I did not actually find it pleasant to look at him—on the contrary I felt resistant to him, he was too superior and cool for me, too provocatively sure of himself, and his eyes had the expression of a grown-up (something children never like), slightly sad, with flashes of mockery within them. Still I could not stop looking at him, whether I liked him or not; whenever he glanced back at me, though, I quickly looked away in alarm. Today when I think back to what he looked like as a student, I can say that he was different in every way from anyone else: he was utterly stamped with his own individual personality, and stood out for that very reason, even though he did everything he could not to stand out. He carried himself like a prince in disguise, living among peasant children and making every effort to seem like them.

He walked behind me on the way home from school. After the other boys went their own ways, he caught up to me and said hello. His greeting, too, was adult and polite, even though he imitated our schoolboy tone when he said it.

"Should we walk a bit together?" was his friendly question. I was flattered, and nodded. Then I told him where I lived.

"Oh, you live there?" he said with a smile. "I know that house. There's something unusual over your front door, it interested me right away."

At first I had no idea what he meant, and was amazed that he seemed to know our house better than I did. There was probably a kind of coat of arms on the keystone over the arch of the doorway, but it had been worn flat over the years and painted and repainted over many times; it had nothing to do with us or our family, as far as I knew.

"I don't know anything about it," I said timidly. "It's a bird or something like that. It must be very old. They say the house used to be part of the monastery."

"That may be," he nodded. "Take a closer look! Things like that can often be very interesting. I think it's a sparrow hawk."

We kept walking, and I was very shy and awkward. Suddenly Demian laughed, as though he had just thought of something funny.

"I was there in your class today," he said in a lively voice. "The story of Cain, with the mark on his forehead. Did you like it?"

No, I rarely liked any of what we had to study, but I didn't dare say that to him—it was like a grown-up was quizzing me. I said I liked it very much.

Demian clapped me on the shoulder.

"You don't need to pretend with me, my friend! But the story is really quite strange, I think, much stranger than most of the things they tell us about in school. The teacher didn't say much about it, of course, just the usual stuff about God and sin and so on. But I think—" He interrupted himself, smiled, and said: "But are you interested?"

He went on: "Yes, well, I think this story of Cain can be interpreted in a totally different way. Most of the things they teach us are no doubt perfectly true and right, but you can see them differently from how the teachers do, and they usually make much more sense when you do that. This Cain with the mark on his forehead, for example, they haven't really explained him to us in a satisfactory way, don't you agree? Someone kills his brother in an argument, that could happen, and then he gets scared and acts innocent, that's plausible too. But for him to be rewarded for his cowardice with a special distinction that protects him and frightens everyone else, that really is very strange."

"You're right!" I said. The topic was starting to get interesting now. "But how else would you interpret the story?"

He slapped me on the shoulder.

"It's simple! The mark came first: that's where the story started. There once was a man with something in his face that frightened people. They were afraid to lay a hand on him, or his children; they were awed. But maybe—in fact, I'm sure of it—there wasn't literally a sign on his forehead like a postmark. Things in life are rarely that obvious. No, it must have been something uncanny, almost imperceptible: a little more spirit, a little more daring in his look than people were used to. This man had power, and others were afraid of that power. He was 'marked.' They could explain it however they wanted, and 'they' always want what's easy and comforting and puts them in the right. They were scared of Cain's children, so the children had 'marks' too. In other words, they explained the mark not as what it really was—a special distinction—but as the opposite. They said that the people with this mark were sinister and unnerving—and so they were. Anyone with courage and character always seems unnerving to others. They felt very uncomfortable having this tribe of fearless, sinister people running around, and so they put a label on them, hung a story around their necks, to get back at them and get some compensation for all the times they had been scared. — You understand?"

"Yes—so you mean—Cain wasn't evil at all? And the whole story in the Bible is actually not true?"

"Yes and no. Ancient stories like that are always true, but they're not always recorded and passed down in the right way. What I think is that Cain was a fine fellow, and they told this story about him because they were scared of him. It was just a rumor, idle gossip. But it was perfectly true, insofar as Cain and his children really did bear a kind of mark and were different from most people."

I was dumbfounded.

"And you think the part about killing his brother isn't all true either?" I asked, gripped with curiosity.

"Oh, that part is definitely true. The stronger one murdered the weaker one. There's no way to know if it was really his brother, but that doesn't really matter, in the end all men are brothers. So, a stronger man killed a weaker man. Maybe it was heroic, maybe not. But in any case the other weaklings were now full of fear, they moaned and complained, and if anyone asked them, 'Why don't you just kill him?' they didn't say: 'Because we're cowards,' they said: 'No one can kill him, he bears a mark. God has marked him!' The lie must have started something like that. — Well, I'm keeping you. Good bye!"

He turned the corner onto Altgasse and left me standing alone, more astounded than I had ever been in my life. Almost as soon as he left, everything he'd said seemed entirely unbelievable to me. Cain a noble person and Abel a coward! The mark of Cain as a badge of honor! It was absurd, it was wicked blasphemy! Where did that leave our Lord? He had accepted Abel's sacrifice, had He not? Did He not love Abel? — No, it

was all stupid. And I had the feeling that Demian was just
making fun of me and trying to trip me up. He was a damned
clever fellow, and he sure knew how to talk, but—no—

At the same time I had never in my life thought so deeply
about any Bible story, or indeed about any story. And I forgot
about Franz Kromer for longer than I had been able to for
some time—I forgot about him for several hours, a whole evening. I reread the story at home, as it was written in the Bible:
it was short and clear; to try to look for a special secret meaning in it was crazy. If Demian was right, every murderer could
claim to be God's chosen one! No, it was nonsense. What I
had liked was just Demian's way of saying these things, so
simple and easy, as though it were all clear and obvious—and
with those eyes of his too!

Of course my own life was not exactly on the right track—
in fact it was on a terribly wrong track. I had lived in a bright,
clean world of light, I was a kind of Abel myself, and now here
I was, stuck fast in the "other" world—I had fallen so far,
sunk so deep, and at the same time there was basically nothing
I could do about it! What was I supposed to make of that?
Then, at that moment, a memory flashed up within me that almost took my breath away: on that ill-starred evening when
my misery had begun, that moment with my father when I
had, so to speak, seen right through him and his bright clean
world and wisdom, and despised them! Yes, I had imagined on
my own that I was Cain and bore the mark, and that the mark
was not a disgrace but a badge of honor; I had felt that my
wicked misdeed made me superior to my father, higher than
the good and pious people in his world.

It's not that I had thought it all through, clearly and analyti-
cally, at the time; it was just an emotion flaring up, strange
stirrings that hurt me but at the same time filled me with pride.
Yet all these ideas were contained in the feeling I'd had.

When I thought about how oddly Demian had spoken of the
fearless tribe and the cowards, how strange his interpretation
was of the mark on Cain's forehead, and how marvelously his
eyes, his peculiar, grown-up eyes, had lit up when he spoke,
the vague thought passed through my mind: This Demian, is

he not himself a kind of Cain? Why else would he defend Cain, if he didn't feel like him? Why does he have such power in his eyes, and why does he speak so scornfully about the "others," the fearful ones, who after all are actually pious and pleasing to God?

I couldn't bring these thoughts to any conclusion, but a stone had fallen into the well, and the well was my young soul. For a long time, a very long time, this whole topic of Cain and the murder and the mark was the starting point for all my efforts at knowledge, all my criticism and doubt.

I noticed that the other students also paid a lot of attention to Demian. I had not breathed a word to anyone about the Cain story and what Demian had said, but he seemed to interest other people too. At least there were a lot of rumors that started circulating about the "new kid." If only I still remembered them now: every one of those rumors would shed some light on him, every one could be interpreted. I remember the first piece of gossip was that Demian's mother was very rich. It was also said that neither she nor her son ever went to church. They were Jewish, someone claimed to know, but then again maybe they were secretly Muslim. In addition, wild tales were told about Max Demian's physical strength. It was a fact that he had horribly humiliated the strongest boy in his class, who had challenged him and called him a coward when he refused to fight. The boys who saw it said Demian had just put one hand on the boy's neck and squeezed until he turned pale; afterward the boy had crept away and not been able to use his arm for days. In fact, word went around one night that the boy was dead. Everything was insisted on as the truth for a while, everything was believed, it was all marvelously exciting. Then, for a while, everyone had had enough. Not long afterward though, new rumors started up—that Demian had had intimate relations with girls and "knew everything."

Meanwhile the situation with Franz Kromer continued on its inevitable course. I could not get free of him; even if he left me alone for days at a time every now and then, I was still tied to him. He was with me in my dreams, like my shadow, and whatever he didn't do to me in real life my imagination had him do to me in these dreams. I was absolutely and completely his slave. I lived more in these dreams than in real life—I had always had powerful dreams—and I lost my strength and life to this shadow. One frequent dream was that Kromer was mistreating me, he spit on me and kneeled on top of me and, what was worse, tempted me into worse and worse crimes—or, rather, he didn't tempt me, he simply compelled me by exerting his powerful influence. The most horrible nightmare, from which I would wake up half insane, involved murdering my father. Kromer sharpened a knife and put it into my hand, we were standing behind the trees on a boulevard and waiting for someone, I didn't know who, and someone came walking by and Kromer squeezed my arm to tell me that this was the person I had to stab, it was my father. Then I woke up.

Although I did think about Cain and Abel in this context, I didn't think much about Demian. The first time he made contact with me again, it was also, strangely, in a dream. Again I was suffering mistreatments and violations in my dream, but this time, instead of Kromer, it was Demian kneeling on me. Also—and this was entirely new, and made a deep impression on me—everything I suffered from and loathed when Kromer did it, I accepted happily from Demian, with a feeling as much of rapture as of terror. I had that dream twice, then Kromer was back again.

It has been a long time since I could separate exactly what I lived through in these dreams from what I experienced in real life. In any case, my bad relations with Kromer took their course, and naturally did not end when I had finally committed enough little thefts to pay off the full amount he said I owed him. Now he knew about all those thefts too, since he always asked me where I had gotten the money from, and so now I was more in his clutches than ever. He threatened again and again to tell my father everything, and almost as great as my fear was the deep regret I felt over not having told my father everything myself, from the beginning. At the same time, however miserable I felt, I wasn't sorry about everything, at least not all the time; sometimes I even thought I felt that everything was the way it must be. A dark fate hung over my head and it was pointless to try to get free of it.

The situation was presumably not a little painful for my parents too. A strange new spirit had come over me; I no longer fit into our group, formerly so warm and intimate, which I often felt a burning desire to return to as though to a paradise lost. I was treated more like a sick child than like an evildoer, by my mother at least, but my true situation could best be seen in how my two sisters acted. Their behavior, extremely considerate and nonetheless utterly upsetting to me, made it very clear that I was some kind of possessed person, more to be pitied than blamed for his condition, but still someone in whom evil had taken up residence. I knew they were praying for me, differently than before, and I felt how useless their prayers were. I often felt a fierce longing for relief and a yearning to confess the whole truth, but I also could tell in advance that I wouldn't be able to explain everything properly, to either my father or my mother. I knew they would accept what I said with love and affection, they would be very gentle with me, even feel sorry for me, but they wouldn't fully understand me and would see the whole thing as a kind of mistake or lapse, when in fact it was destiny.

I know that some people might have a hard time believing that a child, not even eleven years old, could feel such things. My story is not for them. It is meant for people who better understand the human heart. Adults, who have learned to transmute some of their feelings into thoughts, do not see such thoughts in children, so they conclude that the experiences are not there either. But there are very few times in my life that I have lived and suffered as deeply as I did then.

One rainy day, my tormentor had ordered me to come to the Burgplatz. I was standing there, waiting and rooting around with my foot in the wet chestnut leaves that were still falling every now and then from the black, dripping-wet trees. I didn't have any money but had set aside two slices of cake and brought them with me so that at least I could give Kromer something. I had long since gotten used to standing on a corner somewhere, waiting for him, often for a long time. I accepted it the way one always accepts the inevitable.

Finally Kromer arrived. He didn't stay long. He nudged me in the ribs a couple times, laughed, took the cake, even offered me a wet cigarette (which I didn't take), and was friendlier than usual.

"Right," he said when he was leaving, "I almost forgot— next time you can bring your sister with you, the older one. What's her name again?"

I didn't understand him at all and said nothing. I just stared at him in amazement.

"Don't you get it? Your sister, bring her with you."

"Yes, Kromer, but that's impossible. I can't, and she wouldn't come anyway."

I thought this must be another one of his bullying tricks. He used to do that a lot: demand something impossible, scare me, humiliate me, and eventually strike some kind of deal. I had to pay some kind of penalty, money or another offering, for not doing whatever it was.

This time it was different. When I refused, he almost didn't get mad at all.

"Well," he said casually, "you'll think it over. I'd like to meet that sister of yours. It's not hard, you can just take her with you on a little walk, and then I'll show up. I'll whistle for you tomorrow and we'll discuss it again then."

After he left, an idea of what he wanted suddenly dawned on me. I was still a complete child, but I had heard hints and rumors that when boys and girls were a little older they could do some kind of mysterious, indecent, forbidden things with each other. And so now I was supposed to—all of a sudden it was crystal clear to me how monstrous it was! I immediately knew that I would never do it. But what would happen next, how Kromer would take revenge on me—I hardly dared think about it. A new anguish had begun, as if I had not yet been through enough!

I was inconsolable and walked off across the empty square, hands in my pockets. New tortures, new enslavements!

Then a lively, deep voice called my name. I was startled, and set off at a run. Someone ran after me, and a hand grabbed me gently from behind. It was Max Demian.

I let myself be caught.

"It's you?" I said, unsure of myself. "You scared me!"

He looked at me, and never before was his gaze more like that of an adult, a superior being who could see right through me. We had not talked to each other for a long time by that point.

"Sorry," he said in his polite but at the same time firm way. "But you shouldn't get scared like that."

"Yes, well, it happens sometimes."

"Apparently it does. But look: If you flinch like that at someone who hasn't done anything to you, he'll start to think. He'll be surprised; it'll make him curious. This person will think it's strange how jumpy you are, and then he'll think: People are like that only when they're afraid. Cowards are scared of everything. But I don't actually think you're a coward. Are you? Oh, I know, you're not a hero either. There are things you're afraid of; there are people you're scared of too. But that's not right. We should never be scared of anyone. You're not scared of me, are you? Or are you?"

"Oh, no, not at all."

"There, you see. But there are people you're scared of?"

"I don't know. . . . Leave me alone, what do you want from me?"

He kept pace with me—I had started walking faster, thinking I might get away—and I felt him give me a sidelong look.

He started again: "You can assume I mean well. Either way, there's no reason for you to be scared of me. I want to try an experiment with you, it's fun and you might learn something very useful from it. Listen closely! — I sometimes try to do something that people call mind-reading. There's nothing magic about it, but if you don't know how it's done it can seem very mysterious. People sometimes find it quite a shock. — Okay, let's try it. I like you, or I find you interesting, and so I want to bring to the surface your inner way of seeing things. I've taken the first step already: I scared you, which means you're jumpy. So there must be things and people you are afraid of. Now why? There's no reason to be afraid of anyone. If someone is afraid of another person, it's because he has given this person some kind of power over him. For example, maybe he's done something bad, and the other person knows it—then he has power over you. You follow? That's perfectly clear, right?"

I looked him in the face, helpless. His face was as serious and intelligent as ever, and also well-meaning, but without the slightest gentleness—if anything, it was severe. Justice, or something similar, lay in that face. I didn't understand what was happening to me; he stood there like a magician.

"Do you follow?" he asked again.

I nodded. I couldn't say a word.

"I told you it seems mysterious, this 'mind-reading,' but it's perfectly natural. I could also tell you pretty precisely what you thought about me when I told you about Cain and Abel, for example, but that's another topic. I also think you might have dreamed about me once or twice. But enough of that! You're a clever boy, most of them are so stupid—I like to talk to a clever boy once in a while, someone I trust. That's all right with you, isn't it?"

"Oh yes. But, I don't understand how—"

"Let's stay with our fun experiment. So, we've discovered that young S. is jumpy—he is scared of someone—and this someone probably knows an uncomfortable secret about him. Is that more or less right?"

It was like in my dream: I was under his influence, overpowered by his voice. I only nodded. Wasn't he speaking in a voice that could just as well have come from within myself? That knew everything, better and more clearly that I knew it myself?

Demian gave me a sturdy clap on the shoulder.

"So, that's how it is. I thought so. Now just one question: do you know the name of the boy who left the square here before you?"

I was startled and shaken; he had touched on my secret. It

shriveled up painfully inside me, not wanting to come out into the light.

"What boy? There wasn't anyone else, just me."

He laughed.

"Just say it!" he laughed. "What's his name?"

I whispered: "You mean Franz Kromer?"

He gave me a satisfied nod.

"Bravo! You're a quick one, we'll be good friends yet. But now I have something to tell you: This Kromer, or whatever his name is, is a bad person. I can tell from his face that he's a scoundrel. What do you think?"

I heaved a sigh: "Oh yes, he is bad, he is the devil! But he can't find out anything about this! For God's sake, he can't find out! Do you know him? Does he know you?"

"Calm down. He's gone, and he doesn't know me—not yet. But I would very much like to meet him. He goes to the public school?"

"Yes."

"Which grade?"

"Fifth grade. — But don't tell him anything! Please, please, don't say anything!"

"Don't worry, nothing will happen to you. I presume you don't feel like telling me a little about this Kromer?"

"I can't, no, leave me alone!"

He was silent for a while.

"Too bad," he said. "We could have taken our experiment a little further. But I don't want to upset you. But you already know this fear of him isn't right, don't you? Such fear just destroys us, we have to break free of it. You have to break free of it or you will never be all right. Do you understand that?"

"Of course, you're totally right . . . but it's impossible. You don't know. . . ."

"You've seen that I know some things, more than you would have thought. — Do you owe him money?"

"Yes, that too, but that's not the main thing. I can't say it, I can't!"

"So it wouldn't help if I gave you the money you owe him? — I could easily do that."

"No, no, it's not that. And please: don't tell anyone! Not a word! That would be the worst thing that could happen to me!"

"Trust me, Sinclair. Eventually you will tell me the secret you share with him—"

"Never, never!" I shouted.

"As you wish. I only mean that maybe you will decide on your own to tell me someday. Of your own free will, obviously! You don't think I would act like Kromer does?"

"Oh, no—but, you don't know anything about how he acts!"

"Not a thing. I'm just thinking it through. And I'll never do the kind of thing Kromer does, believe me. And you don't owe me anything anyway."

We were quiet for a long time, and I calmed down. But Demian's knowledge grew more and more mysterious to me.

"I'm going home now," he said, and he pulled his loden coat tighter around him to keep out the rain. "There's only one thing I want to tell you, since we've already come this far: You need to break free of him! If there's nothing else you can do, then kill him! I would be impressed if you did, and happy. I'd even help you."

I felt scared again. I suddenly remembered the story of Cain. It was all too sinister for me, and I started to whimper. There was too much uncanniness everywhere around me.

"All right," Max Demian smiled. "Just go home! We'll take care of it. Killing him would be simplest, though, and in situations like this, the simplest thing is always the best. You are not in good hands with your friend Kromer."

I arrived back home, and it felt like I had been away for a year. Everything looked different. There was something standing between me and Kromer now: something like a future, like hope. I was no longer alone! Only then did I realize how terribly alone I had been with my secret for all those weeks and weeks. Right away, what I had thought about so many times before came to mind again: what a relief it would be to confess to my parents, but that it would not resolve everything. Now I had practically confessed to someone else, to an outsider, and a sense of relief came over me like a sweet, strong breeze.

All the same, I was far from overcoming my fear and was still prepared for long and terrible confrontations with my enemy. That made it all the more remarkable that everything proceeded so peacefully, in complete secrecy and calm.

Kromer's whistle in front of our house simply failed to materialize—for a day, then for two days, three days, a week. I couldn't believe it, and secretly I was waiting for him to suddenly show up again after all, just when I least expected it. But he was gone, once and for all! I didn't trust this new freedom and still did not truly believe it, until finally I ran into Franz Kromer himself. He was walking down Seilergasse, straight toward me. When he saw me he flinched, twisted his face into a wild grimace, and turned around on the spot to avoid me.

That was an incredible moment. My enemy fleeing from me! My Satan afraid of me! Surprise and joy flooded through my heart.

Demian turned up again. He was waiting for me in front of the school.

"Hello," I said.

"Good morning, Sinclair. I wanted to hear how you're doing. Kromer's leaving you alone now, isn't he?"

"Did you do it? But how? How?! I don't understand. He's totally gone."

"That's good. If he ever comes back—I don't think he will, but he is quite a scoundrel—then just tell him to remember Demian."

"But what's the connection? Did you start a fight and beat him up?"

"No, I don't like to do that. I just talked to him, the same way I talked to you. I was able to make him see that leaving you alone was to his own advantage."

"Oh, you didn't give him any money, did you?"

"No, my boy. You already tried that approach yourself."

He dodged the question no matter how hard I tried to find out what had happened. I was left with the same awkward feeling toward him, a strange mix of gratitude and shyness, admiration and fear, affection and inner resistance.

I decided to see him again soon; I wanted to talk more with him about everything, including Cain.

It didn't happen.

Gratitude in general is not a virtue I believe in, and it seems wrong to me to demand it from a child. So the complete lack of gratitude I showed to Max Demian does not surprise me all that much. I am absolutely certain today that if he hadn't freed me from Kromer's clutches, my health and in fact my whole life would have been ruined. Even at the time, I felt that this liberation was the greatest event of my young life—but I completely ignored the liberator himself as soon as he had performed the miracle.

Ingratitude, as I said, is not something that needs explaining as far as I am concerned. The only thing I find hard to understand is the lack of curiosity I showed. How could I let a single day go by without trying to learn the secret of how Demian had saved me? How could I rein in my craving to hear more about Cain, more about Kromer, more about mind-reading?

It is almost impossible to believe, and yet it was so. I suddenly found myself freed from a demonic net, and saw the world bright and joyous before me; I no longer suffered from panic attacks and a pounding heart that almost made me throw up. The spell had been broken; I was not a tormented soul in Hell but just a schoolboy again, like before. My nature wanted to regain its equilibrium as quickly as it could, which more than anything meant turning away from all the ugliness and danger I had been through and trying to forget it. With marvelous speed the whole long tale of guilt and terror slipped from my mind, without leaving behind any apparent scars or traces.

The fact that I tried to forget my helper and savior just as quickly makes sense to me now too. I was fleeing, with all the force and might of my damaged soul, from my vale of tears and damnation, from Kromer's terrible enslavement, back to where I had earlier been happy and content: the paradise lost that had opened its gates to me once more, the bright world of Father and Mother, of my sisters—back to the scent of purity, to Abel pleasing in the sight of God.

The very day after my short conversation with Demian, before I was fully convinced my freedom had been won back at last and I did not need to fear any relapse, I did what I had longed so desperately and so often to do: I confessed. I went to my mother and showed her the little money box with the broken lock, filled with play money instead of real coins, and I told her how my own guilt had put me in an evil tormentor's clutches for so long. She did not understand everything I said, but she saw the box and saw my changed look, heard my changed voice, and felt that the trial was over, that I had been returned to her.

Then began the emotional celebration of my coming back into the fold—the return of the prodigal son. Mother took me to see Father, the story was repeated, questions and cries of amazement poured forth, both my parents stroked my head and sighed deeply, free at last of their long dejection. Everything was wonderful, just like in the stories; everything was resolved into magnificent harmony.

I fled into that harmony with true passion. I could not get enough of enjoying my peace and the trust of my parents once more. I was a model child around the house, played more with my sisters than ever before, and felt redeemed as I sang the dear, old hymns during prayer with all the fervor of a convert. All these feelings came from the heart—there was no deception involved.

And yet everything wasn't all right, not at all! This is the only true explanation for why I forgot Demian. I should have confessed to him! That confession would have been less ornamental and moving but more fruitful for me. Instead I was clinging with all my might to the paradisiacal world where I had once belonged; I had come home and been received with mercy. But Demian did not belong to that world in any way, and he could not be made to fit into it. He too—differently from Kromer, but nonetheless—was a tempter; he too was a link between me and the other world, wicked and bad, which I now wanted nothing more ever to do with. I could not and did not want to renounce Abel and glorify Cain, now that I had just turned back into an Abel again myself.

That was my external situation. The inner circumstances,

though, were these: I had been redeemed from Kromer's and the devil's hands, but not through any power or act of my own. I had tried to walk along the paths of the world, and they had proven too slippery for me. And now that a friendly hand had reached out and saved me, I ran straight back, without looking left or right, into Mother's lap, back to the safety of a pious, sheltered childhood world. I made myself younger, more dependent, and more childish than I really was. I had to replace my dependence on Kromer with a new one, because I was unable to walk alone, so I chose, in my blind heart, dependence on Father and Mother, on the old beloved "world of light," even though I already knew it was not the only one. If I hadn't made that choice, I would have had to cling to Demian and put my faith in him. At the time I thought I was unwilling to do so out of a justified mistrust of his outlandish ideas; in truth it was out of nothing but fear. For Demian would have asked more of me than my parents did, much more. He would have tried to make me more independent, with provocations and warnings, mockery and irony. Alas, I now know only too well that there is nothing in the world more hateful to a person than walking the path that leads to himself!

Still, six months or so later I could not resist temptation, and on a walk with my father I asked him what to make of the fact that some people thought Cain was better than Abel.

He was very surprised by the question. He explained to me that this interpretation was in no way new; it had emerged already in the earliest centuries of Christianity and been taught in various sects, one of which called itself the "Cainites." But obviously, he said, this insane teaching was nothing but the devil's attempt to destroy our faith. For if you believe that Cain was in the right and Abel in the wrong, then it follows that God was in error, or in other words that the God of the Bible is not the one true god but a false god. The Cainites and similar sects did in fact teach and preach such a doctrine, but this heresy had long since vanished from the earth. The only thing that puzzled him was that a schoolmate of mine had heard something about it. In any case, he warned me in grave earnest to refrain from all such thoughts.

CHAPTER THREE

THE THIEF ON THE CROSS

There are beautiful, wonderful, tender memories from childhood I could put in this story—my security with Father and Mother, my childhood loves, and my playful, pleasant life in gentle, loving surroundings filled with light. But I am interested here only in the steps I have taken in my life to arrive at myself. I will leave in the glowing distance all the lovely oases, blessed isles, and paradises whose magic I experienced; I have no desire to set foot in them again.

And so, for as long as I stay with my boyhood years, I will speak of only the things that felt new, that pushed me onward, broke me loose.

These prods from the "other world" kept coming up, and every time they brought fear and constraint and bad conscience with them. They always threatened to overthrow the peace in which I would have been happy to remain.

Then came the years when I had to recognize once again a primal drive within me, one that had to cower and hide in the permitted world of light. Like everyone else, I too experienced my slowly awakening sexual feelings as an enemy and a destroyer, as something forbidden, as temptation and sin. The great mystery of puberty, which I was desperately curious to solve and which gave rise to dreams, lust, and fear, did not fit at all in the sheltered bliss of my peaceful childhood world. So I did what everyone does: I led the double life of a child who is no longer a child. My conscious life was lived in the familiar space of what was allowed, and denied the world rising like a new dawn within me. At the same time though, my life was lived in dreams, urges, longings of a subterranean kind across which my consciousness built ever more anxious and fearful bridges as the childhood world within me fell apart. Like almost all parents, mine did nothing to help the life forces awakening within me, which were never spoken about. They only tried, endlessly and untiringly, to help me in my hopeless efforts to deny reality and stay in a child's world that grew more and more false and unreal every day. I do not know if parents can do anything else, and I am not criticizing mine in particular. It was up to me to finish growing up and find my own way; I did it badly, like most well-raised children.

Everyone passes through these difficulties. For the average person, this is the moment when the demands of his life come into the starkest conflict with his environment—when he has to fight hardest to make his way farther along his path. Many people experience the death and rebirth that is the destiny of us all only this once, as childhood rots from within and slowly disintegrates, as everything we have grown to love abandons us, and we suddenly feel the solitude and deathly cold of the universe around us. And very many people remain stuck at this hurdle their whole life long, desperately hanging on to the irretrievable past and clinging to the dream of a paradise lost—the worst and most deadly of all dreams.

Let us return to our story. The sensations and mental images with which the end of childhood proclaimed itself in me are not worth telling here. The important thing was that the "dark world," the "other world," was back. What had once been Franz Kromer was now a part of myself. At the same time, the "other world" outside me was gaining more and more power over me too.

Several years had passed since the incident with Kromer. I felt that that dramatic and guilty period of my life was very far behind me; it seemed like a nightmare that had not lasted long and had vanished without a trace. Franz Kromer had long since ceased to mean anything in my life, to the point that I barely noticed when I did run into him. The other main character in the tragedy, though—Max Demian—never again left my life completely. For a long time he stayed on the margins, in view but not having any effect on me; only gradually did he come closer again, radiating power and influence.

I am trying to recall what I can about the Demian of that time. I may well have said not a word to him for a year or more. I avoided him, and he in no way tried to approach me. The most he would do was nod to me if we happened to run into each other. At such times I sometimes thought I could sense a delicate note of mockery or ironic reproach mixed in with his friendliness, but I may have been imagining it. It was as though the episode I had been through with him, and the peculiar influence he had exerted on me, were completely forgotten, by him no less than by me.

As I try to recall him now, I can see him—he *was* there, and I did notice him. I see him going to school, alone or between two other older students, and I see him walking between the others like an exotic creature, solitary and silent, like a distant star, surrounded by a different air of his own, living under his own laws. No one liked him, no one was close to him, only his mother, and even with her he seemed to behave like an adult, not a child. The teachers had as little to do with him as they could; he was a good student but not eager to please, and now and then we would hear a rumor about something he had supposedly said to a teacher, some comment or backtalk as rude and challenging or sarcastic as could be.

I close my eyes and think back now, and I see his image rise up before me. Where was that? Yes, there he is. It was on the street in front of our house. I saw him standing there one day with a notebook in his hand, drawing. He was drawing the old coat of arms with the bird, above our front door. I stood at a window, hidden behind a curtain, and watched him, and saw, with deep admiration, his keen, cool, bright face turned toward the coat of arms—the face of a man, a scholar or artist, supercilious and purposeful, strangely bright and cold, with knowing eyes.

I see him again. It was a little later, on the street; all of us coming home from school were standing around a horse that had fallen. It lay in front of a farmer's cart, still harnessed to the shafts, and it snorted, complaining and questioning, through wide-open nostrils, and bled from a hidden wound. Dark liquid slowly soaked into the white dust of the street near the horse. When I turned away from the sight, feeling sick, I saw Demian's face. He had not pushed his way to the front; he stood at the back, comfortable with himself and even looking rather elegant, as usual. His gaze seemed directed at the horse's head, again with this deep, silent, almost fanatical but nevertheless dispassionate attentiveness. I could not help looking at him for a long time, and even back then I felt, far from consciously, something very unusual and special about him. I looked at Demian's face and saw the face of a man, not a boy; but not only that, I also thought I could see, or feel, that this was not just the face of a man, it was something else too. There seemed to be something of a woman's face in it as well, in fact the face seemed to me, for a moment, neither manly nor childlike, neither old nor young, but somehow millennial, timeless, marked with different spans of time from the ones we lived in. Animals might look like that, or trees, or stars—I didn't know, I didn't feel precisely what I would say about it now, as an adult, but I felt something like that. Maybe he was beautiful, maybe I was attracted to him and maybe repelled too, there was no way to decide that either. I saw only that he was different from us—he was like an animal, or like a spirit, or like a picture, I don't know what he was but he was different, unimaginably different from us all.

My memory tells me nothing more. Maybe this scene too is partly made up of later impressions.

Only when I was several years older did I finally come back into closer contact with him. Demian had not been confirmed in church with the rest of his class, as was customary; here too all sorts of rumors had immediately sprung up. It was whispered once again around school that he was a Jew, or, no, a heathen, and still other students were sure he was an atheist, his mother too, or a member of some kind of legendary, evil sect. I feel like I also heard people say they suspected he and his mother were lovers. In any case he had presumably not been raised religiously up until then, but they must have decided this might cause problems for his future, so his mother decided to have him confirmed after all, two years later than the other boys his age. That is how it happened that he was my classmate for months in confirmation class.

For a while I avoided him entirely. I did not want any part of him, completely shrouded as he was in rumors and secrets. The truth, though, was that what bothered me was the feeling that had stayed with me since the Kromer affair: that I owed him something. And I was busy enough with my own secrets just then. For me, confirmation class coincided with the period of decisive revelations in sexual matters, and, despite my best efforts, these revelations interfered drastically with my interest in religious instruction. The things the pastor spoke of lay at a great distance from me, in a silent, sacred unreality; however beautiful and valuable they were, they were not at all urgent or exciting, while these other matters possessed those qualities in the highest degree.

The more this circumstance made me indifferent to confirmation class, the more interested I became in Max Demian again. There seemed to be some kind of bond between us. I need to retrace this connecting thread as carefully as I can. As far as I can recall, it first formed in class early one morning, when the lights were still turned on in the schoolroom. Our religious instructor had arrived at the story of Cain and Abel. I paid hardly any attention; I was sleepy, barely listening. Then the pastor raised his voice and began speaking forcefully about the mark of Cain. At that moment I felt a kind of touch or admonition. I looked up and saw Demian's face turned toward me from the front row of desks, with a bright, meaningful look in his eye, an expression which might have been either mocking or serious. He looked at me for only a moment, and suddenly I was listening intently to what the pastor was saying; I heard him talk about Cain and his mark, and felt the knowledge, deep inside me, that what he was teaching was not how it really was, that it was possible to look at it differently, that criticism was possible!

From that moment on, the connection between Demian and me existed once again. And, strangely, no sooner was this feeling of a spiritual bond there in the soul than it was almost magically transposed into physical space as well. I didn't know if he had done it or if it was pure chance—back then, I still believed in chance—but after a few days Demian had suddenly moved to a different seat in religion class, directly in front of me. (I still remember how happy I was, surrounded by the horrid morning air of an overfilled schoolroom that reeked like a poorhouse, to breathe in the fresh clean smell of soap from his neck!) After another couple days he had changed seats again and was now sitting next to me, and that was where he stayed, through the winter and all spring.

The class was entirely transformed. It was no longer soporific and boring. I looked forward to it. Sometimes we both listened to the pastor with the greatest interest—one glance from my neighbor was enough to call my attention to a remarkable story or strange proverb. And another glance from him—a very particular kind of glance—was enough to put me on alert and awaken my doubt and critique.

Often, though, we were bad students who didn't listen at all. Demian always behaved well around his teachers and fellow students—I never saw him playing schoolboy pranks or laughing out loud or whispering in class; no teacher ever had to reprimand him. But he knew how to communicate with me, more with silent signs and glances than with words. And the thoughts and ideas he shared with me were sometimes very strange.

He told me, for example, which of the students he found interesting and how he was studying them. He had very exact knowledge about some of them. For example he would tell me before class: "When I give you a signal with my thumb, so-and-so will turn around to look at us," or scratch his neck, or whatever it was. Then during class, usually when I had almost forgotten about it, Max would suddenly turn to me and make a conspicuous gesture with his thumbs and I would quickly look at the student he was pointing to, and every time I saw him making the predicted gesture like a puppet on a string. I nagged Max to try it on the teacher sometime, but he didn't want to. One time, though, when I came to class and told him

I hadn't done my homework, and that I really hoped the pastor would not call on me, he helped me. The pastor looked around for a student to recite a section of the catechism, and his roving gaze rested on my guilty face. He slowly came over, stretched out his finger toward me, already with my name on his lips—and then suddenly looked confused or distracted, tugged at his collar, walked over to Demian, who was looking him straight in the face, and seemed to want to ask him something, but unexpectedly turned away again, coughed once or twice, and called on someone else.

These games amused me very much; I noticed only gradually that my friend often played the same kind of trick on me. It happened sometimes on my walk to school that I would suddenly have the feeling that Demian was walking behind me, and when I turned around, there he was.

"Can you really make other people think what you want?" I asked him.

He readily answered, calmly and objectively in his usual adult manner.

"No," he said, "no one can. Because we do not have free will, even if the pastor pretends we do. Other people can't think what they want, so I can't make them think what I want. But it is possible to observe someone closely enough that you can say, sometimes rather precisely, what he's thinking or feeling, and then you can usually predict what he's about to do. It's very easy, people just don't know how. It takes practice, of course. Let me give you an example. Among butterflies there are certain species where the females are much rarer than the males. They reproduce just like other animals, with the male fertilizing the female, which lays eggs. Now if you have a female of one of these species—scientists have tested this many times—the males come flying toward this female all night, sometimes from hours away. Hours, just think! From miles and miles away, these males feel the presence of the only female in the area! People have tried to explain the phenomenon, but it's difficult. They must have a kind of special sense of smell or something, the same way good hunting dogs can pick up and follow imperceptible traces. Do you understand? Na-

ture is full of such things that no one can explain. Now I say:
if the females were as common as the males, this species of
butterfly would not have such a sensitive sense of smell! They
have it only because they've trained themselves to have it. If an
animal, or a person, directs his whole attention and will at a
particular thing, he attains it. That's all it is. And it's the same
with what you're thinking. If you look at someone closely
enough, you will know more about him than he knows himself."

The word "mind-reading" was on the tip of my tongue, I
was about to utter it and remind him of the incident with
Kromer that lay so far in the past. But that was another odd
thing between us: neither he nor I ever, ever made the slightest
reference to this decisive intervention he had made in my life.
It was as though there had never been anything between us, or
as though each of us firmly believed the other had forgotten it.
Once or twice we even ran into Franz Kromer when we were
walking down the street, but we exchanged not a glance, not a
word about him.

"What do you mean about free will?" I asked. "You say we
don't have any, but then you say that you only have to direct
your will firmly toward something and you'll get it. That
doesn't make sense! If I'm not the master of my own will, then
I can't direct it here or there however I want."

He clapped me on the shoulder. He always did that when I
pleased him in some way.

"It's good you asked!" he said with a laugh. "It's important
to always ask, always doubt. But the answer is very simple. If
one of our butterflies tried to direct his will toward a star or
something, he couldn't do it. It's just—he never tries to. He
seeks out only what has value and meaning for him, what he
needs, what he absolutely must have. And then the unbelievable happens, he develops a magical sixth sense that no other
animal has! We humans have a wider range, certainly, and
more interests than an animal, but we too are stuck in a rela-
tively narrow circle and cannot break free of it. Of course I
can imagine this or that, decide that I absolutely have to reach
the North Pole or what have you, but I can will it strongly

enough to actually accomplish it if the wish lies entirely in my self, if it truly, completely corresponds to my nature. When that happens, when you try to follow a command from within, then it works, you can harness your will like a good work-horse. For example, if I got the idea into my head that I wanted to make our pastor stop wearing glasses, it wouldn't work. That would just be playing games. But back in the fall, when I made the firm decision to be moved from my desk up in front, it worked perfectly. Suddenly someone showed up who had been sick until then, he was ahead of me in the alphabet, and since someone had to move to make room for him, it was nat-urally me who did it, because my will was ready to take the opportunity as soon as it came up."

"Yes," I said, "it felt very strange for me too. As soon as you and I took an interest in each other, you came closer and closer. But how? You couldn't sit next to me right away, you sat a few rows ahead of me first, didn't you? Then what hap-pened?"

"It was like this: When I first felt the urge to move, I didn't quite know where I wanted to go, I only knew that I wanted to sit farther back. My will to sit next to you was there, but I wasn't conscious of it yet. At the same time, your will was ex-erting its force and helped me. Only when I was sitting right in front of you did it occur to me that my wish was only half-fulfilled—I realized what I actually wanted all along was to sit next to you."

"But no new student showed up that time."

"No, but I just did what I wanted and sat down next to you. The boy whose place I took was surprised, but what was he going to do? He moved. The pastor noticed that something had changed—in fact every time he calls on me or looks at me, something secretly bothers him, he knows my name is Demian and that it's wrong for a D to be sitting all the way back here with the S's—but it never forces its way into his consciousness, because my will opposes it, and I always prevent it from hap-pening. He keeps noticing something is wrong, and he looks at me and starts to study me more carefully, the good man, but every time that happens I do the same simple thing. I look him very, very straight in the eye. Almost no one can take that well. They all get nervous. If you want something from someone, and you look him straight in the eye and he doesn't get uncomfortable at all, then give up! You'll never get what you want from him, never! But that very rarely happens. In fact, I only know one person this strategy doesn't work on."

"Who?" I asked quickly.

He looked at me with the slightly narrowed eyes he always had when he was thinking about something. Then he looked away and didn't answer, and despite my burning curiosity I was unable to repeat the question.

But I think he meant his mother. — He apparently lived on very close terms with her, but he never talked to me about her and never invited me over to his house. I barely knew what his mother looked like.

Back then, I sometimes tried to do what he did and direct my will so powerfully toward something that I would have to achieve it. I certainly had wishes that felt urgent enough to me. But nothing happened; it didn't work. I couldn't bring myself to talk to Demian about it either. I wouldn't have been able to admit to him what I wanted. And he also didn't ask.

My religious faith had meanwhile developed certain gaps. Still, I felt that there was a big difference between my own thinking, completely influenced as it was by Demian, and that of my unbelieving fellow students. There were some who occasionally let slip a comment about how ridiculous and beneath our dignity it was to believe in a god, how fairy tales like the trinity or Jesus's immaculate birth were simply laughable, and how it was a scandal in this day and age for anyone still to peddle such nonsense. Those were in no way my views. Even if I had my doubts, the whole experience of my childhood had taught me enough about the reality of a pious life, a life like my parents', to know it was neither undignified nor hypocritical. I had the deepest respect for religion, the same as before. It was just that Demian had gotten me to start seeing and interpreting the stories and doctrines in freer, more personal, playful, and imaginative ways; at least I always followed with pleasure and delight the interpretations he laid out for me. A lot of it was more than I could accept, of course, like the business about Cain. One time in confirmation class he shocked me with an idea that was even more radical, if that was possible. The teacher had told us about Golgotha. The Biblical account of the Savior's suffering and death had always made a very deep impression on me, as far back as I can remember; sometimes as a young boy, for instance on Good Friday after my father had read me the story of the Passion, I would live, deeply and inwardly moved, in that sorrowful, beautiful, pale and spectral yet monstrously vital world, in Gethsemane and on Golgotha, and when I heard Bach's *St. Matthew's Passion* the whole dark majestic glow of suffering in that mysterious world filled me with overpowering, mystical shudders. I still think this music and the "Actus tragicus" are the epitome of all poetry, all artistic expression.

At the end of class, Demian said rather thoughtfully: "There's something I don't like about that story, Sinclair. Read it through again, and test it out on your tongue: there's something about it that leaves an insipid taste in your mouth. It's the part about the two thieves. It's magnificent, of course, those three crosses standing next to one another on the hill! But then this sentimental little tract about the good thief! He used to be a criminal, he's committed God knows what crimes, and now he gets all mushy and performs these whiny rituals of self-improvement and repentance?! What's the point of remorse if you're two steps away from the grave, I ask you? It's nothing but a sanctimonious fairy tale, treacly and dishonest, insipid and sentimental and obviously didactic. If you met those two thieves today and had to pick one of them as your friend, or decide which of the two to trust, it's completely obvious you wouldn't pick the weepy convert. You'd pick the other one—he's someone with character. He thumbs his nose at converting, which in his case would be nothing but pretty talk anyway; he follows his path to the end and doesn't chicken out at the last minute, doesn't try to talk his way out of what he owes the devil, who must have helped him up until then. He has character, all right, and people of character don't come off too well in Bible stories. Maybe he's another descendant of Cain. Don't you think?"

I was aghast. I had believed myself entirely at home in the story of the Passion, and only now did I see how little I had engaged with the story personally, how little imaginative power I had brought to bear when I heard it and read it. That said, Demian's new idea sounded sinister, possibly fatal; it threatened to overturn certain notions I had whose continued existence I felt I had to cling to. No, you couldn't just play around with anything and everything, even the most sacred!

As always, he noticed my resistance right away, even before I said anything.

"I know," he said, resigned. "It's the same old story: Whatever you do, don't take what it says seriously! But there's something I want to tell you. This is one of the places where you can clearly see the flaws in this religion. This whole God, in the Old Testament and the New Testament both, is a marvelous character, true, but he's not what he's supposed to be. He is good and noble, the Father, the high and beautiful, the sentimental—all true! But the world consists of other things too. And all those other things get chalked up to the devil; that whole part of the world, that whole half, is just suppressed and hushed up. The same way God is praised for being the Father of all life, while everything sexual, everything life in fact depends on, is simply hushed up or described wherever possible as the devil's work, and sinful! I have nothing against honoring and worshipping this God Jehovah, not in the least. But I think we should honor everything, and worship everything— the whole world is sacred, not just this artificially partitioned official half! We need not only church service but a devil's service. That's what I think. Or else we need to create a God who includes the devil too, and whose eyes we don't need to cover when the most natural things in the world take place in front of him."

He spoke with an intensity, almost violence, that was unusual for him, but he smiled as soon as his speech was done and did not push his point any further.

In me, though, these words struck at the riddle of my whole adolescence, which I carried within me every hour of every day, and about which I had never spoken a word to anyone. What Demian had just said about God and the Devil, about the godly official world and the hushed-up devilish world, was precisely my own idea, my own myth: the idea of the two worlds, or half-worlds, one of light and one of darkness. The realization that my problem was one that every person had—a problem affecting all life and all thought—came over me like a holy shadow, and I saw, and suddenly felt, with fear and awe, how deeply my innermost life and thoughts were a part of the eternal river of great ideas. This realization was not a happy one, although it did give me a certain satisfaction. It was hard—it left a harsh taste in my mouth—because a note of responsibility resounded in it, a sense of no longer being able to remain a child. Of standing alone.

I told my friend—it was the first time in my life I had revealed such a deep secret—about the idea I had had since my earliest childhood, about the "two worlds," and he immediately saw that by doing so I was agreeing with him from the depths of my heart. But he was not the type to take advantage. He heard me out, paying me the same close attention he always had, and looked me in the eye until I had to turn away. For once again I saw in his gaze that strange, animalistic timelessness and unfathomable age.

"We'll talk more about it another time," he said gently. "I can see you're thinking about more than you can say. But whenever that's the case, then you haven't fully lived what you've thought—as you know—and that is not good. Only a thought we've lived has any value. You knew that your 'permitted world' was only half the world, but you've tried to suppress the other half the way the pastor and teachers do. It won't work! It never does for anyone who has started to think."

This struck a deep chord in me.

"But still, there are truly forbidden and ugly things," I almost screamed, "you can't deny that! They are not allowed, and we have to not do them. I know that people commit murder and do all kinds of vicious things, but does that mean I'm supposed to go turn into a criminal?"

"We won't be done with this today," Max said soothingly. "Of course you shouldn't rape or murder anyone, no. But you can't really see yet what is 'allowed' and what is 'forbidden'—you're not there yet. You have only felt a first piece of the truth. The rest will come, don't worry! For example, you've had an urge in yourself, for a year or so, that is considered 'forbidden.' The Greeks, on the other hand, and many other peoples too, considered this urge a God, and they honored it in great festivals. In other words, 'forbidden' is not an eternal truth—it can change. Today, anyone is allowed to sleep with a woman as soon as he's been to a pastor with her and married her. It's different with other peoples, even today. And so every one of us has to find out for himself what is allowed and what is forbidden—forbidden to him. It is entirely possible to never do anything forbidden and still be an absolute scoundrel. And vice versa. — Really, it's just a question of comfort! Anyone too comfortable to think for himself and be his own judge simply obeys the laws as they are. He has it easy. Other people feel commandments inside themselves—things are forbidden to them that upstanding citizens do every day, and other things are permitted to them which are usually frowned upon. We all have to stand on our own."

Suddenly he seemed to regret having said so much, and he broke off. Even then I could understand to a certain extent, emotionally, why he felt that way. He may have expressed these ideas in a casual, sociable way, but actually he was sick to death of talking "just for the sake of conversation," as he once put it. He could feel my real interest in these matters, but also too much game-playing, too much enjoyment of clever chit-chat, or something along those lines—in short, my lack of complete seriousness.

As I re-read these last words I have written—"complete seriousness"—I suddenly remember another scene, my most vivid experience with Max Demian in that period when I was still half a child.

Our confirmation was approaching, and the final topic we covered in our religion class was the Last Supper. It was an important theme for the pastor and he made a great effort to get through to us; we could feel a certain solemnity of mood in those final sessions. But in just those classes my thoughts were elsewhere—in fact they were on my friend. Confirmation had been explained to us as the ceremonial entrance into the community of the church, but as it approached I could not help thinking that the value for me of this semester of religious instruction lay in not what we had studied but rather the proximity and influence of Demian. I was now prepared to enter not into the church, but into something quite different: an order of thought and of personality that had to exist somewhere on earth. I considered my friend its representative, or ambassador.

I tried to suppress this thought—it meant a lot to me to celebrate my confirmation with a certain dignity, despite everything, and I found it hard to do so with my new ideas. And yet whatever I did, the thought was there, and it gradually became linked in my mind with the upcoming church ceremony. I was ready to celebrate it differently from the others; for me it would signify an entrance into the world of ideas I had come to know through Demian.

It was during that period, right before class one time, that I again got into a vigorous argument with him. My friend didn't say much and did not seem pleased with my speeches, which in truth were probably rather pompous and self-important.

"We're talking too much," he said with unusual seriousness. "There is no point in clever talk, none at all. It only leads you away from yourself. Going away from yourself is a sin. What a person needs to do is crawl entirely into himself, like a turtle."

Just then we entered the schoolroom. Class started, I tried to pay attention, and Demian did not distract me. After a while I began to feel something strange emanating from next to me, where he was sitting: a coldness, or emptiness, or something like that, as though the seat had unexpectedly ceased to be filled. When the feeling became oppressive, I turned my head.

I saw my friend sitting up straight, with his usual good posture. But nonetheless he looked entirely different from how he usually did, and he gave off something, was surrounded by something, that I hadn't ever felt. I thought he had closed his eyes but saw he still had them open. But those eyes didn't look, they were not seeing, they were glassy and directed inward or at something very far away. He sat there completely motionless, appearing not even to breathe; his mouth was as though carved of wood or marble. His face was pale, uniformly pale, like stone, and his brown hair was the most living thing about him. On the desk in front of him lay his hands, lifeless and still like objects, rocks, or fruit, pale and motionless but not limp— like good, sturdy shells around a strong hidden life.

I trembled at the sight. He's dead! I thought, and I almost said it out loud. But I knew he wasn't dead. I stared spellbound at his face, at that pale, marble mask, and I felt: that is Demian! The way he usually was when he walked and talked with me was only half of him—a Demian playing a temporary role, adapting himself to others and going along with things for the sake of politeness. The true Demian, though, looked like this: stony, ancient, like an animal, like marble, beautiful and cold, dead and secretly full of tremendous life. And all around him this silent emptiness, this ether and outer space, this loneliness of death!

He has entirely gone into himself now, I felt with a shudder. I had never felt so abandoned. No part of him had stayed with me; he was unreachable; he was farther away than if he had been on the most remote island in the world.

I could hardly believe no one saw it but me. Surely everyone had to look over at him, everyone should be shuddering at the sight! But no, no one paid any attention to him. He sat rigid as a statue—I could not help but think: as an idol. A fly landed on his forehead and walked slowly across his nose and lips, and he didn't twitch a muscle.

Where was he, where? What was he thinking, what was he feeling? Was he in some kind of Heaven, or a Hell?

There was no way I could ask him about it. When I saw him living and breathing again, at the end of class, when his eyes met mine, it was like before. From where had he returned? Where had he been? He looked tired. His face had color again, his hands moved again, but his brown hair was now dull and seemed tired.

For the next few days I repeatedly tried a new exercise in my bedroom: I sat rigid on a chair, made my eyes glassy, kept completely still, and waited to see how long I could last and what I would feel. All that happened was that I felt tired, and my eyelids itched terribly.

Not long afterward was the confirmation. I have no significant memory of it.

Then everything changed. Childhood fell to pieces around me. My parents looked at me with a certain embarrassment. My sisters had turned into totally alien creatures. A kind of disillusionment made all the feelings and joys I was used to seem faded and unreal; the garden no longer smelled sweet, the woods were no longer tempting, the world lay spread out all around me like a clearance sale of old, useless things, boring and unappealing. Books were just paper, music just noise. It was like how an autumn tree sheds its leaves: the tree feels nothing, the rain runs off it, or the sun, or the frost, and the life inside it slowly withdraws into its narrowest, innermost places. It does not die. It waits.

It had been decided that I would be sent to a different school next year and live away from home for the first time. Every so often during that summer, Mother would treat me with special tenderness, saying goodbye in advance, intent on conjuring up love and homesickness in my heart, and unforgettable memories. Demian had left on vacation. I was alone.

CHAPTER FOUR

BEATRICE

When vacation was over, I went to St.— without having seen my friend again. Both my parents came with me and entrusted me with all possible care to a boy's boarding house run by a teacher at the high school. They would have frozen with horror had they known the kind of life they were letting me wander into.

The question was still whether I would, with time, turn into a good son and useful citizen, or whether my nature was pushing me onto other paths. My last attempt to be happy under the shadow of the parental house and its spirit had lasted a long time—for a while it had almost succeeded, but now it had finally and completely failed.

The strange emptiness and isolation I had come to feel for the first time the summer after my confirmation (and oh, how well I got to know it later—this emptiness, this thin air!) did not pass away so quickly. I found it oddly easy to leave home— I was a little ashamed of not being sadder, in fact; my sisters cried inconsolably, but I couldn't. I was amazed at myself. I had always been a sensitive child who expressed his feelings— a good boy, when it came down to it. Now I had completely changed. I acted with total indifference toward the outside world and spent days at a time attending only to myself, listening to the dark, forbidden, underground currents rushing and roaring inside me. I had shot up very quickly in the past six months and looked lanky, skinny, and immature. Everything boyishly lovable about me had disappeared; I was well aware that it was impossible to love me as I was, and I did not love myself either. I missed Max Demian much of the time, and desperately wished he were there, but I not infrequently hated him too and held him responsible for the impoverishment of my life that I accepted as an ugly disease.

At first I was neither liked nor respected in our student boarding house; the other boys teased me and then left me alone, having decided I was a weird, distant, unpleasant sort. I took pleasure in this identity and even exaggerated it, grumbling my way into a solitude that looked like manly superiority and contempt on the outside while secretly I suffered constant fits of depression and despair. At school I got by for a while on what I had already studied back home—the class was a bit behind where we had been—and I got into the habit of viewing the other students my age with a certain contempt, as children.

It went on like that for over a year. Nothing changed on my first few visits home, and I was always glad to go back to school.

Then it was early November. Whatever the weather, I would take little intellectual walks, which often gave me a kind of pleasure that was full of melancholy, scorn for the world, and contempt for myself as well. That was how I felt one evening as I strolled through the city in the damp, misty twilight. The wide avenue of a public park was completely deserted, and inviting; as I walked down the lane, thickly covered with fallen leaves, I shoveled my feet around in the leaves with a dark, voluptuous desire. It smelled wet and bitter; distant trees loomed up eerily out of the mist, tall and shadowy.

I stopped at the end of the avenue, not knowing what to do next. I stared down at the dark vegetal mass and greedily breathed in the wet smell of death and decay, which something inside me responded to and welcomed. Oh, how insipid the taste of life was!

Someone approached down a side path, his coat billowing in the wind. I wanted to keep walking, but he called my name.

"Hallo, Sinclair!"

He came up to me. It was Alfons Beck, the oldest student at our boarding house. I always enjoyed seeing him and had nothing against him except that he always treated me in an avuncular, ironic way, the same as he did everyone younger than him. He was said to be as strong as a bear, he had the teacher who ran our boarding house under his thumb, and he was the hero of numerous high-school rumors.

"And what brings you here?" he called out affably, in the tone that bigger kids liked to take when they condescended to talk to one of us. "Writing a poem, I bet."

"Never occurred to me," I snapped back.

He laughed out loud and walked next to me, chatting. I had completely forgotten what that felt like.

"Don't think I wouldn't understand, Sinclair. I know how it is, when you're taking a walk like this in the evening mist, with autumn thoughts, you want to write poems, I know. Poems about dying nature, of course, and the lost youth it's a symbol of. Heinrich Heine and all that."

"I'm not that sentimental," I defended myself.

"All right, never mind! Anyway, in weather like this it does you good to find a nice quiet place with a glass of wine or something along those lines. You want to come with me? I happen to be all alone at the moment. — Or would you rather not? I don't want to lead you astray if you're planning to be a model schoolboy."

Soon we were sitting in a small pub at the edge of town, drinking a dubious wine and clinking our thick glasses together. I didn't like it very much at first, but still it was something new. Soon though, not used to drinking wine, I started talking my head off. It was as though a window had opened inside me, and the world was shining in—how long, how terribly long it had been since I'd said anything I really felt! I started to give my imagination free rein, and before I knew it I was telling Beck the story of Cain and Abel.

Beck listened with delight. Finally, someone to whom I had something to give! He clapped me on the shoulder, he called me a devil of a fellow, and my heart swelled with pleasure: I could finally let myself go, indulge in the need to talk and communicate that had been pent up for so long, and feel acknowledged by someone older, like I was worth something. When he called me a brilliant little bastard, what he said sank into my

soul like sweet, strong wine. The world shone in new colors—
thoughts came to me from a hundred mischievous sources—
wit and fire blazed up within me. We talked about our teachers
and classmates, and it seemed to me we understood each other
splendidly. We talked about the Greeks, and paganism, and
Beck insisted on turning the conversation to confessions of
amorous adventures. Here I had nothing to contribute. I had
not had any adventures, nothing worth telling. And what I
had felt, had built up in my imagination, burned within me
but the wine did not free it or enable me to talk about it. Beck
knew a lot more about girls than I did, and I listened passion-
ately to his fairy-tale stories. What I learned was unbelievable:
things I had never thought possible entered ordinary reality
and seemed obvious, normal. Alfons Beck, eighteen years old
or so, had already acquired quite a store of experience. Among
other things, that girls always want nothing but chivalry and
attention, which is fine as far as that goes but not the real
thing. You could get farther with women. They were much
more reasonable. Frau Jaggelt, for example, who ran the store
that sold pencils and notebooks for school—you could really
talk to her, and as for what's gone on behind the counter in her
store, no book in the world could describe everything.

I sat there in a trance, stupefied. Not that I could ever love
Frau Jaggelt—but still, this was incredible news. It seemed that,
at least for older people, there were wellsprings of pleasure that
I had never dreamed of. At the same time I heard a false note in
his stories—it all seemed narrower and pettier than true love
would feel, in my opinion—and yet it was reality, it was life and
adventure, and sitting right next to me was someone who had
lived it, to whom it seemed perfectly natural.

Our conversation had sunk to a lower level somehow; it had
lost something. I was no longer the brilliant little fellow either,
just a boy listening to a man's stories. But even so—compared
to what my life had been for months and months, this was delicious, it was paradise. It was also, I gradually started to feel,
very much against the rules: the whole thing, from sitting in a
pub to what we were talking about. At least for me it was a
real taste of rebellion, of spirit.

I remember that night very clearly. When the two of us started home late, past the dully burning gas lamps in the cool wet night, I was drunk for the first time. It did not feel pleasant—it was excruciating, actually—but still, there was something about it: sweet excitement, rebellion, spirited life. Beck took good care of me, even while griping about what a total beginner I was, and he brought me home, half carrying me, and managed to smuggle us into the house through an open hall window.

But after a short dead sleep, I woke up to a headache, sobriety, and terrible sadness. I sat up in bed, still wearing my shirt from the day before, with my other clothes and shoes lying around on the floor and stinking of smoke and vomit. Between headache, nausea, and unspeakable thirst, an image rose up in my soul that I had not seen for a long time: I saw my parents' house, my hometown, Father and Mother, my sisters, the garden; I saw my quiet, comfortable bedroom, the school and the market square, saw Demian and our confirmation classes—all of it flooded with bright light, radiant, all of it wonderful, godly, and pure, and I now knew that everything, everything, had still belonged to me the day before, just a few hours ago, had been waiting for me for return, but now, only now in this moment, it had sunk forever under the waves, was cursed, was no longer mine. It had thrown me out and now looked upon me with disgust! Everything I had so profoundly loved, everything back to the most distant, golden garden of childhood my parents had given me—every kiss from Mother, every Christmas, every bright, pious Sunday morning at home, every flower in the garden—it was all laid to waste, I had trampled it all under my feet! If a band of henchmen had come at that moment and bound me hand and foot, leading me to the gallows as a scapegoat, a desecrator of the temple, I would have gone uncomplainingly, even gladly, gone and found it only just and right.

So that's how I looked on the inside! I, who went around despising the world, proud in spirit, and pretending to think Demian's thoughts along with him! I was a pig, like scum, drunk and filthy, disgusting and low, a wild animal taken unawares and overpowered by hideous urges. I, who had come from the garden where everything was purity and radiance and blessèd tenderness, who had loved beautiful poetry and Bach, now looked like that inside. I could still hear my laugh ringing in my ears—drunk and out of control, bursting out in idiotic stops and starts—and it filled me with outrage and disgust. That was me!

Despite everything, it was almost pleasurable to suffer these torments. I had crept around blind and numb for so long, my heart cowering poor and miserable in the corner, that even this self-hatred, this horror, this whole horrible feeling in my soul was welcome. At least I felt something! The embers still flickered with some kind of fire, a heart still beat in there! I was confused to feel something like liberation and springtime in the middle of all my misery.

Meanwhile, to the outside world, things went downhill with me in a hurry. My first binge was soon only the first of many. A lot of drinking and running wild went on in our school, and I was one of the very youngest students to join in; before long I was no longer merely a tolerated novice but a ringleader, a star of the scene: a notorious, reckless barfly. Once again I belonged entirely to the dark world—to the devil—and in that world I was considered a splendid fellow.

At the same time, I felt miserable. I was living in a self-destructive riot of sensuality, and while my schoolmates saw me as a leader, a devil of a fellow and a damned sharp and clever guy, deep inside me hid a timid soul fluttering with fear. I can still recall how tears came to my eyes once when I left a bar on a Sunday afternoon and saw children playing in the street, bright and happy, with freshly combed hair, in their Sunday clothes. And the whole time that I was entertaining and often shocking my friends with my monstrous cynicism at the dirty tables of cramped pubs between puddles of beer, in my heart of hearts I still respected what I was mocking. On the inside I kneeled in tears before my soul, before my past and my mother, before God.

I never felt truly one with my companions—I was still lonely when I was with them, and that was why I suffered so. There was good reason for this: I was a barroom hero, a scoffer to satisfy the roughest of the rough; I showed spirit and courage in what I thought and said about our teachers, school, parents, church; I could take the dirtiest jokes and even offer a few of my own—but I never went along with my buddies to see girls. I was alone, and full of a burning longing for love—a hopeless longing even while I talked like a hardened libertine. No one was more fragile, more full of shame, than I was. And every now and then, when I saw the young girls from good families walking down the street, pretty and clean, light and cheerful, they seemed like wonderful, pure dreams, a thousand times too good and pure for me. For a long time I couldn't set foot in Frau Jaggelt's stationery store either, because I turned red when I looked at her and remembered what Alfons Beck had told me.

The more I realized how lonely and different I would always be in my new circle too, the harder it became for me to break free of it. I don't know anymore if all that drinking and show-ing off ever brought me any real pleasure; I also never learned to hold my liquor well enough to avoid suffering painful con-sequences the next day. It was all like some kind of compul-sion. I did what I had to do because I had no idea what else I could try. I was afraid of spending so much time alone, and anxiously ashamed of the warm, shy moods I so often felt, the tender thoughts of love that so often came over me.

What I missed most was a friend. There were two or three schoolmates I enjoyed seeing, but they were good, well-behaved students, and my vices were long since common knowledge. So they avoided me. Everyone saw me as a reckless daredevil, on thin ice. My habits were no secret to the teachers either, and I was often seriously punished; it was generally ex-pected that I would be kicked out of school before long. I knew it myself—I had stopped being a good student a long time ago—but I laboriously scraped by and conned my way through, with a feeling that it could not go on like this much longer.

There are many ways in which the god can make us lonely and lead us to ourselves. This was the path he took with me.

It was like a bad dream. I see myself under the spell of some kind of dream, crawling restless and tormented through the dirt and sticky muck, through broken beer glasses and nights spent cynically chattering away—an ugly and unclean path. There are dreams like that, where on the way to a princess you stay stuck in a pool of shit, or a stinking back street full of filth. That's how it was with me. It was given to me to grow lonely in this undignified way, and to place between myself and my childhood the gates of Eden, closed forever and watched over by implacable, radiant guards. It was a new beginning, and the awakening of a hopeless longing for my former self.

Still I was startled and I shook with fear the first time my father turned up unexpectedly in St.—, alarmed by my host's letters from the boarding house. When he visited again, around the end of that winter, I was already hard and indifferent, and I let him scold me, plead with me, appeal to my memories of Mother as much as he wanted. By the end he was utterly enraged and said that if I didn't change he would let me be kicked out of school in disgrace and send me to reform school. Well, let him! When that second visit ended and he left, I felt bad for him, but he had accomplished nothing—he could no longer find a way to reach me, and sometimes I felt that it served him right.

As for what would become of me, I couldn't care less. In my odd and unpleasant way, sitting in bars and acting full of myself, I was fighting against the world—it was my form of protest. In the process I only wore myself out, but I sometimes saw it like this: If the world has no use for people like me, if it can find no better place or higher task for them, then so much for us. But it would be the world's loss.

Christmas vacation that year was anything but happy. My mother was horrified when she saw me again—I had grown even taller, and my scrawny face looked gray and wasted, with slack features and inflamed rings around my eyes. The first hints of a moustache, and the glasses I had recently started to wear, made me look even less like the boy she knew. My sisters kept their distance, giggling. It was painful. The conversation

with Father in his study was painful, and bitter; the greetings
of a few relatives, painful; Christmas Eve, especially painful.
For as long as I could remember, that had been the great day in
our house—the night of festivity and love, of gratitude, of re-
newing the bonds between myself and my parents. This time it
was all depressing, even embarrassing. As usual my father read
the Gospel passage about the shepherds "keeping watch over
their flock by night"; as usual my sisters stood beaming with
delight next to the table with their presents on it; but my father's voice sounded unhappy, and his face looked old and
pinched, and my mother was sad, and to me the whole thing
seemed embarrassing and unnecessary: the presents and the
Christmas wishes, the Gospel and the tree. The gingerbread
smelled delicious and gave off thick clouds of even more delicious memories. The tree smelled and told of things that no
longer existed. I longed for the evening, and the holiday, to
come to an end.

It went on like that all winter. I had recently been given a severe warning by the teachers' council and threatened with expulsion. It would not be long now. Well, fair enough.

I especially resented Max Demian. I had not seen him again
during this whole period; I had written to him twice, when I
had started school at St.—, but not received an answer. That
was why I did not go to see him during vacation.

At the start of spring, when the thorny hedges were just starting to turn green, I happened to notice a girl in the park where
I had run into Alfons Beck the previous fall. I was taking a
walk by myself, full of unsavory thoughts, and worried: my
health had taken a turn for the worse, and aside from that I
was constantly short of money, owed my classmates money,
and had let my tabs in various stores, for cigars and such
things, get quite large. I had to invent unavoidable expenses to
get my parents to send me more from home. Not that I felt any
of these worries very deeply—if my time here was about to
come to an end, and I was about to either drown myself or get
sent to reform school, these trivial details would never matter.

Still, I was constantly living face to face with unpleasant things, and I suffered from it.

That spring day in the park, I saw a young lady I found very attractive. She was tall and thin, elegantly dressed, and with an intelligent boy's face. I liked her right away—she was the type I loved, and she soon began to fill my imagination. She was probably not that much older than me but was much more polished, elegant, and clearly defined, almost a lady already, but with a hint of exuberance and boyishness in her face that I liked enormously.

I had never yet managed to approach a girl I had fallen for, and I failed with this one too. But she made a deeper impression on me than any other girl ever had, and the effect this infatuation had on my life was powerful.

Suddenly I had an image before me again—a high and noble image I respected, and oh, how I wanted to worship and adore! There was nothing I thirsted for more deeply and strongly. I named her Beatrice, because without having read Dante I already knew about Beatrice from an English painting I had a reproduction of. It showed an English Pre-Raphaelite female figure, long-limbed and slender, with a long, thin face and spiritual hands and features. My beautiful girl from the park didn't look exactly like her, but she too had the same slender boyishness of form that I liked, as well as some of the same refined or soulful quality in her face.

I never said a single word to Beatrice. And yet, she had the deepest possible influence on me at that time. She held up an image before my eyes, showed me something sacred, turned me into a worshipper in a temple. Overnight I was finished with drinking and staying out late. I was able to spend time alone again; again I could enjoy reading and going for walks.

This sudden conversion earned me more than my fair share of mockery, needless to say. But I didn't care: I had something to love and adore—I had an ideal, and life was again full of promise and mysterious colors in the twilight. I felt comfortable with myself, although only as a slave beholden to an honored image.

I cannot think back to that time without feeling moved.

What I was trying to do, as sincerely and fervently as I knew how, was rebuild another "world of light" from the rubble of a shattered period of my life; my whole life was centered around the desire to throw off everything dark and evil in myself, to dwell completely in the light, on my knees before the gods. At least this time the "world of light" was my own creation, to some extent. I was no longer running away, back to Mother and a sense of security without any responsibility; now I was serving something new, invented and summoned forth from myself, and demanding a certain responsibility and self-discipline. The sexuality I suffered from and was constantly fleeing could now be transformed into spirit and reverence in this holy fire. I was free of everything dark and ugly—no more nighttime groans, no more looking at obscene pictures with my heart pounding, no more listening in at forbidden doors, nothing dirty at all. Instead I built myself an altar, to the image of Beatrice, and by dedicating myself to her I was consecrating myself to the spirit and the gods. I took back a portion of life from the dark powers and offered it up to the powers of light. My goal was not pleasure but purity; not happiness but beauty and spirit.

This cult of Beatrice completely changed my life. From one day to the next, the premature cynic had become an acolyte with only one goal: to become a saint. I not only threw off the wicked life I had grown accustomed to, I tried to change everything—I wanted to bring purity, nobility, and dignity into everything I did, whether eating or drinking, my words or my clothes. I started every morning with cold ablutions; at first I had to force myself, but then they came naturally. I behaved seriously and with dignity, stood up straight, walked slower and with more dignity. It may have looked from the outside like ridiculous affectation, but to me it felt like nothing less than the service of God.

Of all the practices I embarked on to express my new way of thinking, one became especially important for me. I started to paint. At first, it was because the English picture of Beatrice I had did not resemble my Beatrice closely enough—I wanted to try to paint her for myself. With an entirely new feeling of joy and hope, I brought beautiful paper, paints, and brushes into my room (I had a room of my own by that point) and prepared a palette, a glass, porcelain bowls, and pencils. The fine tempera paints in little tubes that I had bought delighted me. They included a fiery chromium oxide green, and I can still see it lighting up my little white bowl for the first time.

I was cautious at first. It is hard to paint a face, and I wanted to start by trying other things. I painted ornaments, flowers, and little imaginary landscapes—a tree by a church, a Roman bridge with cypresses. Sometimes I lost myself entirely in this playful activity, as happy as a child with his paint box. Finally, though, I started to paint Beatrice.

Several efforts were total failures and I threw them away. The more I tried to capture the face of the girl I still saw on the street every now and then, the worse it went. Finally I gave up and started to simply paint a face from my imagination, following wherever the paint and brush led me. What emerged was a dream-face, and I was not unsatisfied with it. But I immediately tried again, and each new picture spoke to me more clearly and came closer to the type, if in no way closer to reality.

I got more and more comfortable drawing lines and filling surfaces with a dreaming brush, playfully feeling my way forward, the pictures not following any model but arising from the unconscious. At last, one day, almost without any conscious effort, I finished a face that spoke to me more powerfully than any of the others had. It was not the face of the girl from the park—but I had long since stopped trying to make it be. It was something else, something unreal but no less valuable for that. It looked more like a boy's face than a girl's; the hair was not light blond, like my pretty girl's, but reddish brown, and the chin was firm and strong, though the mouth glowed a vivid red; the whole face was somewhat stiff and mask-like, but impressive and full of inner life.

As I sat before the finished picture, it made a strange impression on me. It struck me as a kind of idol or icon or sacred mask—half masculine, half feminine; ageless; strong-willed and dreamy at once; rigid and at the same time secretly vital and alive. This face had something to tell me—it belonged to me—it demanded something of me. And it bore a certain similarity to someone, though I didn't know who.

This portrait accompanied all my thoughts for some time; it shared my life. I kept it hidden away in a drawer so that no one would find it and make fun of me, but as soon as I was alone in my room I took it out so it could keep me company. At night I pinned it up to the wallpaper across from me, over my bed, so that I would see it as I fell asleep and first thing when I woke up the next morning too.

It was just then that I started to dream a lot again, the way I always had as a child. I felt like I hadn't had any dreams for years. Now they were back, with dream-images of an entirely new kind, and the portrait I had painted showed up in these dreams over and over again: living and talking, my friend or my enemy, sometimes grimacing grotesquely and sometimes infinitely noble, harmonious, and beautiful.

One morning when I woke up from one of these dreams, I suddenly recognized the face. It looked at me with such marvelous familiarity and intimacy, as though it were calling my name. It seemed to know me like a mother, seemed to have been turned toward my face since the dawn of time. I stared at the sheet with my heart pounding—at the thick brown hair, the half-feminine mouth, the strong and oddly bright brow (it had dried like that on its own)—and I felt recognition, rediscovery, and knowledge coming closer and closer to me.

I leaped out of bed, stood before the face, and looked at it up close—stared right into the wide-open, greenish, fixed eyes, the right one slightly higher than the left. And suddenly that right eye twitched, lightly and delicately but clear as day, and with that flutter I recognized the image. . . .

How could it have taken me so long! It was Demian's face.

Later I compared the page many times with Demian's actual features as I remembered them. They were not the same, although they were similar. But still, it was Demian.

One time, on an early summer evening, the red sunlight was slanting through my west-facing window. A dim twilight entered the room. I had the idea of pinning the portrait of

Beatrice, or Demian, to the wooden cross between the panes of the window and seeing how it looked with the evening sun shining through it. The face became blurred, losing all its outlines, but the red around the eyes, the bright forehead, and the intensely red mouth glowed deep and savage from the paper's surface. I sat across from it for a long time, even after the light was gone. The feeling gradually came over me that this was not Beatrice, and not Demian, but rather—myself. The picture didn't look like me—and it wasn't supposed to, I felt—but it was my life, it was my soul, my destiny, my daemon. That was how my friend would look, if I ever found another friend; that was how my lover would look, if I ever found her. That was how my life would be, and my death—it was the sound and the rhythm of my destiny.

I had recently started reading a book that made a deeper impression on me than anything I had ever read. I would rarely encounter another book in that way ever again, either, maybe none but Nietzsche's. It was a book by Novalis, with letters and aphorisms, many of which I did not understand, but they all attracted me and drew me in anyway. One of the maxims came back to my mind, and I wrote it under the portrait with a quill: "Fate and character are different names for the same idea." Now I understood what it meant.

I saw the girl I called Beatrice many more times. I no longer felt nervous excitement when this happened, only a gentle harmony, a presentiment rich in emotion: you are joined to me, but not you, only your image; you are a part of my destiny.

I started to feel a great longing for Max Demian again. I had not heard anything about him for years and had seen him only once on my vacations. Thinking back, I see I have omitted this short meeting in my account here, out of what I now see was shame and vanity. I have to make up for that omission.

So, on one vacation from school during my bar-hopping phase, when I was wandering around my hometown with the same blasé and half-asleep face I always had then, swinging my walking stick and seeing philistines in all the old unchanged faces of the fellow townspeople I despised, my former friend came up to me. I flinched almost as soon as I saw him. Lightning-fast, the memory of Franz Kromer came to me. How I hoped that Demian had forgotten that whole story! It was so unpleasant to have this debt to him—really it was just stupid childhood nonsense, but still, it was something I owed him. . . .

He seemed to wait and see if I wanted to say hello to him, and when I did, as casually as I could, he held out his hand to me. There it was again, his handshake! So firm, so warm and yet cool, and so manly!

He peered into my face and said, "You've grown up, Sinclair." He himself seemed completely unchanged to me: still as old, still as young, as ever.

He joined me, and we walked together talking about nothing but trivial matters—nothing about the past. I remembered I had written to him several times without receiving an answer. Oh, let him have forgotten that too, those stupid, idiotic letters! He said nothing about them.

There was no Beatrice yet, and no portrait; I was still in the midst of my dissolute time. Before we got back to the city, I invited him to a pub. He agreed. Showing off, I ordered a bottle of wine, poured him a glass, toasted with him, and showed him how well acquainted I was with student drinking customs. I emptied the first glass in a single gulp.

"You go to bars a lot?" he asked me.

"Oh, yes," I said lazily. "What else is there? In the end it's still the most fun thing to do."

"You think so? It may be. Some parts of it are great—the euphoria, the Bacchanalian side. But it seems to me that most people who spend a lot of time in bars have lost all that. Running round to bars all the time is what's truly philistine. Now staying up all night once, with torches lit, in real drunkenness and frenzy, that's one thing. But again and again, one glass after another, that's not the real thing, is it? Can you imagine Faust as a regular in some bar night after night?"

I drank my wine and gave him a hostile look.

"Yes, well, we can't all be Faust," I said curtly.

He looked at me a little suspiciously.

Then he laughed his old cool and superior laugh.

"Let's not fight about it! In any case, a drunkard's or sensualist's life is presumably more lively than a blameless middle-class life at least. Also—I read somewhere—the life of a sensualist is one of the best preparations there is for mystics. It's always people like St. Augustine who turn into visionaries. He was a rake and a sensualist beforehand too."

I was suspicious, and wanted at all costs to avoid bowing down to him and his lessons. So I said, in a blasé voice, "Yes, well, to each his own. To tell you the truth, I have no interest in becoming a visionary or whatever."

Demian looked knowingly at me from his slightly narrowed eyes.

"My dear Sinclair," he said slowly, "I wasn't trying to say anything disagreeable. And anyway—neither of us really knows the real reason why you're drinking. Whatever it is inside you shaping your life knows already. It's so good to know that there's something inside us, and that it knows everything, wants everything, and does everything better than we do! — But forgive me, I have to go home now."

We said brief goodbyes. I stayed at the bar in a bad mood, drank my whole bottle of wine, and then, when I got up to go, found out that Demian had already paid for it. That annoyed me even more.

I could not stop thinking back to this little incident. It was Demian to a T. And the words he had spoken in that bar on the edge of town came back to my mind, strangely fresh, as though he had just said them: "It's so good to know that there's something inside us, and that it knows everything, wants everything, and does everything better than we do!"

How I longed to see Demian. I didn't know anything about him and had no way to reach him. I knew only that he was probably at university somewhere, and that his mother had left our hometown after he'd graduated high school.

I tried to call up all my memories of Max Demian, even back to my history with Kromer. So many things he had said to me echoed in my ears then, all still meaningful, still current, still relevant to me! What he had said about the sensualist and the visionary at our last meeting, unsatisfactory as it had been, suddenly stood shining before my soul too. Wasn't that exactly what had happened with me? Hadn't I lived in drunkenness and filth until a new vital urge brought the exact opposite to life within me—a desire for purity, a longing for the sacred?

I continued to pursue my memories. Night had long since fallen, and it was raining outside. In my memories I heard the rain too—it was that time under the chestnut tree when he had first asked about Franz Kromer and guessed my first secrets. One scene after the other rose up in my mind: conversations on the way to school, confirmation classes. Last of all, my very first meeting with Max Demian came to mind. What had we talked about again? I couldn't recapture it right away, but I plunged completely into the past and waited as long as it took, and then it came back to me—that too. We were standing in front of my house after he'd told me his ideas about Cain, and he was saying something about the old, faded coat of arms above our door, in the keystone that grew wider at the top than it was at the bottom. He said it interested him, and that you should pay attention to such things.

That night I dreamed about Demian and the coat of arms. It changed from one thing into another in a continual metamorphosis while Demian held it in his hands: now it was small and gray, now multicolored and tremendously large. He explained to me that it nevertheless remained always one and the same. Finally he made me eat it. When I swallowed it, I felt, with monstrous horror, that the bird on the coat of arms I had swallowed was still alive inside me—it filled me entirely and started to eat away at me from the inside. I was terrified I would die, and I started up in bed.

Soon I was fully awake. It was the middle of the night, and I could hear the rain coming into my room. I stood up to close the window and stepped on some pale thing on the floor. In the morning I realized it was my painting. It lay in a puddle on the floor and had gotten warped and bent. I smoothed it out and put it between sheets of blotting paper in a heavy, thick book. When I looked at it again the next day, it was dry. But it had changed. The red mouth was paler and thinner. Now it was exactly Demian's mouth.

I decided to paint another picture, of the heraldic bird. I no longer knew exactly what it looked like, and I knew that some of its features could not be made out even if you stared right at it from up close, since the thing was old and had been painted over many times. The bird was standing or sitting on something, maybe a flower, or a basket or nest, or the crown of a tree. I didn't worry about it and started with what I had a clear mental picture of. Some inchoate need compelled me to start with strong, bright colors—in my picture, the bird's head was golden yellow. I worked on it as the mood took me, and finished it in a few days.

It had turned into a bird of prey, with the aquiline, pointed head of a sparrow hawk. Half of its body was stuck inside a dark globe that it was working its way out of, as though out of a giant egg. The more I looked at the picture, the more it seemed like the brightly colored coat of arms I had seen in my dream.

There was no way I would have been able to write a letter to Demian, even if I'd known where to send it. I decided, though, in the same dreamlike intuitive state with which I did everything at that time, to send him the picture of the sparrow hawk, whether or not it would ever reach him. I did not write anything on it, not even my name; I carefully trimmed the edges of the paper, bought a large envelope, and wrote my friend's former address on it. Then I mailed it off.

An exam was approaching, and I had to work harder than usual at my schoolwork. The teachers had taken me back into their good graces, ever since I had changed my contemptible ways. Not that I was a good student even now, but neither I nor anyone else still thought about how close I had been to expulsion only six months before.

My father was writing to me again, the same way as before, without threats or recriminations. But I felt no urge to explain to him or anyone else how my transformation had taken place. It was purely by chance that the change coincided with the wishes of my parents and teachers. It did not bring me any closer to them, or to anyone—it only made me lonelier. It was aiming in another direction: at Demian, at a distant fate, I myself didn't know yet, I was still in the middle of the transformation. It had started with Beatrice, but I had been living with my paintings and my thoughts of Demian for so long, in such an unreal world, that she too had vanished utterly from my eyes and my thoughts. There was no one I could say anything to about my hopes, my dreams, my inner transformation, even if I had wanted to.

And how could I have wanted to?

CHAPTER FIVE

THE BIRD FIGHTS ITS WAY OUT OF THE EGG

My painted dream-bird was on its way, in search of my friend. Then, in the strangest way, an answer came back to me.

One day in class, after a break between lessons, I found a note stuck in the book on my desk. It was folded exactly the way my classmates typically folded the notes they would occasionally pass during class; I wondered only who might have given it to me, since I had never had that kind of friendship with any of my classmates. I thought it must be an invitation to join in on some kind of schoolboy prank, which I wouldn't do anyway, and I stuck the note unread in the front of my book. Only later, during the lesson, by chance, did my hand come across it again.

I played with the sheet of paper, unfolded it without thinking, and found a few words written inside. I glanced at it, my eyes rested on one of the words, and I read the note in shock while my heart clenched as though freezing cold at this new turn of fate:

"The bird fights its way out of the egg. The egg is the world. Whoever wants to be born must destroy a world. The bird flies to god. The god is called Abraxas."

I read these lines over and over and sank deep into thought. There could be no doubt: it was an answer from Demian. No one knew about the bird except him and me. My picture had reached him. He had understood and was helping me interpret it. But how did everything fit together? And—what tormented me most of all—what did "Abraxas" mean? I had never heard or read the word before in my life. "The god is called Abraxas!"

The lesson went by without my hearing a word. Then the next class started—the last class of the afternoon. It was taught by a young assistant teacher, Doctor Follen, only recently out of university; we liked him for just that reason, because he was so young and didn't put on airs with us.

He was taking us through Herodotus—one of the few subjects in school that truly interested me. But this time I couldn't pay any attention to it. I had mechanically opened my book, but I didn't follow the translation and remained sunk in thought. Incidentally, I had already confirmed for myself, many times over, how true what Demian had told me in confirmation class was: whatever you wanted strongly enough happened. Whenever I was deeply occupied with my own thoughts during class, I could relax and know the teacher would leave me alone. If you were distracted or drowsy, then he would suddenly be standing there, true: that had happened to me as well. But when you were really concentrating, really lost in thought, you were protected. I had also tried out his trick of the fixed stare and found it reliable too. Back when I was in school with Demian, it had not worked for me; now I often had reason to feel that there was a lot you could do with your gaze and with your thoughts.

That time too, I sat there a million miles away from Herodotus and from school. But then the teacher's voice unexpectedly shot into my consciousness like a bolt of lightning and I snapped awake in panic. I heard his voice, he was standing right next to me, and I even thought he had called my name. But he was not looking at me. I breathed easier.

Then I heard his voice again. It loudly pronounced the word: "Abraxas."

Doctor Follen went on with his explanation, the beginning of which I had missed: "We must not imagine the views of these ancient sects and mystic communities as naïve, the way they might seem from a rationalistic perspective. Science in our sense of the word was unknown to Antiquity, but in return they engaged in a very advanced way with philosophical and mystical truths. These pursuits gave rise to magic spells and other such trickery, to some extent, and no doubt to crime and deception often enough too. But even this magic had a noble heritage and embodied profound thought. For example, the teachings of Abraxas I just mentioned. This name is mentioned in connection with Greek magic formulas and is often considered the name of some kind of magical devil, like the ones savage tribes still believe in today. But Abraxas seems to mean much more than that. We can think of the name as referring to something like a deity whose symbolic task is to unite the divine and the satanic."

The erudite little man eagerly went on with his splendid lecture. But none of the students paid much attention, and since the name did not come up again, I too soon turned my attention back to myself.

"To unite the divine and the satanic": the words resounded within me. Here was a place to start. I was familiar with that idea from the conversations I'd had with Demian in the last phase of our friendship. He had said that the god we worshipped represented only an arbitrarily sectioned-off half of the world (the official, permitted world, the "world of light"). But we should worship the whole world, so either we needed a god who was also the devil, or we needed to establish devil's services along with the church services that honored God. — And so here was the god who was devil and god in one: Abraxas.

I eagerly tried to follow this trail for some time, but I didn't get anywhere. I rummaged through whole libraries looking for more information about Abraxas, without success. Well, my nature was never one for this consciously directed seeking, the kind where at first you find only truths that lie in your hand like a dead weight.

The figure of Beatrice I had thought so much and so deeply about for a time now gradually subsided, or rather strode slowly away from me, getting closer and closer to the horizon and becoming ever more shadowy, pale, and distant. She no longer satisfied the longings in my soul.

Then a new formation began to emerge in the life I was

strangely both sleepwalking through and spinning inside myself. A longing for life blossomed within me, or rather a longing for love. The sexual urges I had been able to dispel for a while with my worship of Beatrice began to clamor for new objects, new images. Again it found no fulfillment, but I was even less able than before to deny these feelings, or hope that the girls my schoolmates used to try their luck with might satisfy them. Again I had intense dreams, and the truth was I dreamed them more by day than at night. Ideas, images, or wishes rose up in me and pulled me away from the outside world, to the point where my relationship with these pictures inside me, these dreams and shadows, were truer and more vital than those I had with my true surroundings.

One particular recurring dream or play of the imagination became very meaningful for me. It was the most important and lasting dream of my life, and it went something like this: I was returning to my father's house—the heraldic bird glowing yellow on a blue background above the door—my mother came up to me from inside the house, but when I went in and tried to hug her it wasn't her, it was someone I had never seen, big and powerful, resembling Max Demian and the picture I had painted but different from them, and absolutely, completely feminine, despite its great power. This figure pulled me to her and took me in a deep, trembling embrace. Bliss mingled with horror—the embrace was in the service of god and also a terrible crime. There was too much about the figure wrapping me in her arms that recalled my mother, too much too that recalled my friend Demian. Her embrace violated every kind of reverence and was nonetheless blissful salvation. I often woke up from this dream with a deep sense of happiness, often in deathly terror and with a tortured conscience, as though I had committed a horrible sin.

Only gradually and unconsciously did this entirely interior image start to seem linked to the hint I had received from without about the god I should seek. But then the link grew tighter and deeper, and I began to feel that this dream-premonition was nothing other than a summoning of Abraxas. Bliss and horror, man and woman blended together, the most sacred holiness intertwined with the most hideous abomination, deep guilt flashing through the loveliest innocence—such was the image I saw in my sex dream and so too was Abraxas. Love was no longer either the dark, animalistic drive I had fearfully felt it to be at first, or the pious, spiritual worship I had offered up to the image of Beatrice. It was both—both and much more: angelic and Satanic, man and woman in one, human and animal, the highest good and the uttermost evil. To live this love seemed to be my destiny, to taste of it my fate. I longed for it and was terrified of it at the same time, but it was always there, always above me.

The next spring I was due to graduate high school and go to university, although I did not know where, nor what I should study. I had a thin moustache on my upper lip; I was a grown man, and yet utterly aimless and helpless. My only certainty was the voice within me, the dream image. I felt a duty to follow its lead, blindly. But it was hard, and every day I rebelled against it again. Maybe I was crazy, I often thought—maybe I was not like other people. . . . Still, I could do everything the others did, without much effort: read Plato, solve trigonometry problems, follow a chemical analysis. There was only one thing I couldn't do: wrest the darkly hidden goal from inside me and see it before me, the way the others did, the ones who knew they wanted to be professors or lawyers, doctors or artists, who knew how long their path would take and what advantages it would bring. That was what I could not do. Maybe I too would become one of those things someday, but how could I know? Or maybe I would search and search for years, and nothing would come of me, I would reach no goal at all. Or maybe I would reach a goal, but it would turn out to be wicked, dangerous, terrible.

All I wanted to do was try to live the life that was inside me, trying to get out. Why was that so hard?

I tried many times to paint the love-image from my dream in all her power. I never succeeded. If I had, I would have sent the picture to Demian. Where was he? I didn't know. I knew only that he and I were linked. When would I see him again?

The happy tranquility of the weeks and months of my Beatrice period were long since gone. At the time I thought I had reached an island of peace, but it was always the same—no sooner had I gotten used to a situation, no sooner had a dream helped me a little, then it too shriveled and went blind. No use complaining! Now I was living in a raging fire of unsatisfied longings and tense waiting that often left me completely wild, almost insane. I saw the image of my dream lover before my eyes, clearer than life—much more clearly than I could see my own hand. I talked to it, cried before it, cursed it; I called it Mother and kneeled before it in tears, called it Beloved and foresaw its ripe, all-fulfilling kiss, called it devil and whore, vampire and murderer. It lured me into the most tender and beautiful dreams, and into vile shamelessness; nothing was too good and precious for it, nothing too low and bad.

I spent that whole winter in an inner turmoil I find hard to describe. I had long since grown used to solitude, so I was not oppressed by loneliness: I lived with Demian, with the sparrow hawk, with the image of the tremendous dream-shape that was both my fate and my beloved. That was enough for me, because everything in my life looked out into vast open spaces, everything pointed to Abraxas. But none of these dreams and thoughts were mine: I could not summon them up at will or give them whatever color I wanted. They came and took possession of me; I was ruled by them, my life was lived by them.

At least I had nothing to fear from the outside world—I was not afraid of anyone and my schoolmates knew it too. They treated me with a furtive respect that often made me laugh. I could see right through most of them whenever I wanted, and I sometimes startled and amazed them by doing so. But I rarely or never wanted to. I cared only about myself, always myself. But I desperately yearned to someday, at long last, live a little too: to put something of myself out into the world; to struggle against, and connect with, that world. Sometimes, wandering the streets at night, too restless to go back home before midnight, I thought that now, now, I would have to see my beloved, crossing the street at the next corner or calling to me from the next window. At other times my whole existence felt

like unbearable torture, and I was prepared to take my own
life.

Then I found a strange refuge—by "chance," as they say.
But there is no such thing as chance in such matters. When
someone needs something and then finds what he needs, it is
not chance that has put it in his hands: rather he himself, his
own longing and need, leads him to it.

Two or three times on my walks through the city, I had
heard organ music from a small church at the edge of town. I
hadn't stopped, but the next time I passed by I heard it again
and recognized the music as Bach. I walked up to the gate,
which was locked, and since the road was almost empty of
people I sat down on a bollard next to the church, pulled the
collar of my coat around me, and listened. It was not a great
organ, but it was a good one, and it was being played marvelously, with a strange, highly personal expression of will and
insistence that made it sound like a prayer. I had the feeling:
That man knows about a buried treasure hidden in this music,
and he is wooing and pounding and striving with all his might
for this treasure like his life depended on it. I do not understand much about music, in a technical sense, but ever since I
was a child I have instinctively understood this expression of
the soul, and felt musical things inside me as natural and self-
evident.

Then the organist played something modern, maybe Max
Reger or someone like that. The church was almost completely
dark, with only a very thin light coming out of the nearby window. I waited until the music was over, then paced back and
forth until I saw the organist leave the church. He was still
young, but older than I was, stocky and burly in shape, and he
walked quickly away, with powerful but somehow reluctant
footsteps.

From that point on I sat or walked back and forth in front of
the church every now and then. One time I found the door
open and sat in the pews for half an hour, shivering and happy,
while the organist played up above in the poor light of a gas
lamp. In every piece of music he played, I heard more than the
piece itself—it seemed as though everything he played was re-

lated, mysteriously connected. Everything he played was religious, was devotional and pious, but not pious like the churchgoers and the pastors—it was pious like pilgrims and beggars in the Middle Ages, unconditionally devoted to a feeling for the world that transcends all creeds. The old masters who came before Bach were played often, and old Italians. And all of them said the same thing, said what the musician had in his soul too: yearning, a sincere grasping at the world combined with desperately cutting oneself off from it, a fervent hearkening to one's own dark soul, the frenzy of devotion and a profound curiosity about the miraculous.

One time, when I secretly followed the organist after he left the church, I saw him go into a little tavern a long way from the center of town. I couldn't resist—I followed him in. I got my first good look at him. He was sitting at a table in a corner of the small room, a black felt hat on his head and a jug of wine in front of him. His face was just as I had expected: ugly and a little wild, searching and inflexible, stubborn and willful, but soft and childlike around the mouth. All the masculinity and strength of that face lay in the eyes and the brow; the lower half of the face was delicate and unfinished, lacking in self-control, almost effeminate, the chin indecisive and boyish as though in protest against the forehead and the gaze. I liked his dark brown eyes, full of ferocity and pride.

I sat down across from him without a word. There was no one else in the bar. He looked at me as though trying to make me go away, but I stood firm and looked back at him, unblinking, until he grumbled: "What are you staring at? What do you want from me?"

"I don't want anything from you," I said. "But I've already gotten a lot from you."

He furrowed his brow.

"So, you're a music enthusiast? I think it's disgusting when people go into raptures about music."

I didn't let him scare me off.

"I've listened to you play in the church many times," I said. "I don't want to disturb you, by the way. I just thought I might find something in you, something special, I don't know exactly what. But don't pay any attention to me! I can just listen to you in the church."

"I always lock up."

"You forgot to, the other day, and I sat inside. Usually I stand outside, or sit on the bollard."

"Really? You can come inside next time, it's warmer. Just knock on the door. But knock hard, and not while I'm playing. And now, out with it—what are you trying to say? You're a very young man, probably in high school or university. Are you a musician?"

"No. I like to listen to music, but only the kind you play—absolute music, the kind where you can feel someone rattling the gates of Heaven and Hell. I think I like music because it has so little to do with morality. Everything else is moral or immoral, and I am looking for something that isn't. Morality has only ever made me suffer. I'm not expressing myself very well. — Did you know that there needs to be a god who is god and devil at once? I have heard it said that there once was a god like that."

The musician pushed his wide hat back on his head and shook his dark hair off his broad forehead. He leaned over the table toward me and gave me a penetrating look.

With bated breath he asked: "What is the name of this god you are talking about?"

"I hardly know anything about him, actually nothing except his name. He is called Abraxas."

The musician looked around suspiciously, as though someone might be eavesdropping. Then he moved closer to me and said in a whisper: "I thought so. Who are you?"

"I'm a student at the high school."

"How do you know about Abraxas?"

"By chance."

He pounded the table with his fist so hard that some wine spilled out of his glass.

"Chance! Don't talk such sh— . . . , such nonsense, young man! No one has heard of Abraxas by chance, you know that yourself. I will tell you more about him. I know a little about him."

He fell silent and slid his chair back. As I looked at him expectantly, he made a face.

"Not here! Another time. — Here, have some."

He reached into the pocket of his coat, which he hadn't taken off, and pulled out a couple roasted chestnuts that he tossed at me.

I didn't say anything. I took them, ate them, and was satisfied.

"So!" he whispered after a while. "How did you hear of . . . him?"

I did not hesitate to tell him.

"I was alone and didn't know what to do," I said. "Then I remembered a friend from years ago, who was very wise, I thought. I had painted something, a bird coming out of a globe. I sent it to him. After a while, when I had stopped really believing I would hear from him, I found a sheet of paper that said: The bird fights its way out of the egg. The egg is the world. Whoever wants to be born must destroy a world. The bird flies to god. The god is called Abraxas."

He didn't respond. We peeled our chestnuts and ate them with wine.

"Should we have more wine?" he asked.

"No, thank you. I don't like to drink."

He laughed, a bit disappointed.

"As you wish! I don't feel that way. I'll stay here. Now go!"

The next time I went to hear him play the organ, he didn't say much. He took me up an old alleyway and led me through a stately old house into a big, rather dark and desolate room, where there was nothing to suggest music except a piano, while a large bookcase and writing desk gave the room an intellectual air.

"You have so many books!" I said with admiration.

"Some of them are my father's library. I live here with him. — Yes, young man, I live here with my father and mother, but I can't introduce you to them. My acquaintances do not meet with much respect in this house. My father is an extremely honored citizen of this city, an important pastor and preacher. And just so you know, I am his gifted and promising son who unfortunately went off the rails, and to some extent mad.

I was a theology student, but just before my exams I left that upright discipline. Actually, though, I still do study that field, at least in terms of my private reading. I have always found the kinds of gods that people have come up with in different places and times an extremely interesting and important topic. Anyway, I am a musician now, and it looks like I will be given a modest position as an organist soon. Then I'll be back in the church after all."

I scanned the spines of the books and saw Greek, Latin, and Hebrew titles, as far as I could tell in the weak light of the little desk lamp. Meanwhile my new acquaintance had lain down on the floor near the wall in the dark and was doing something there.

"Come here," he called after a while, "we're going to do a little philosophy now. That means keep your mouth shut, lie on your stomach, and think."

He struck a match and lit the paper and wood in the fireplace he was lying in front of. The flames shot up and he fanned and fed the fire with exceptional care. I lay down next to him on the threadbare carpet. He stared into the fire, which soon absorbed me too, and we lay there in silence on our stomachs in front of the flickering wood fire for probably an hour, watching it blaze and roar, writhe and subside, flutter and flicker, and finally brood on the bottom of the fireplace in a silent, sunken glow.

"Fire worship was not the dumbest idea anybody ever had," he murmured at one point to no one in particular. Other than that, neither of us said a word. With my eyes fixed on the fire, I sank into dream and silence, saw shapes in the smoke and images in the ashes. One time I was startled: when he threw a piece of resin into the embers a narrow little tongue of fire shot up, and I saw in it the bird with the yellow sparrow hawk's head. Golden glowing threads ran together into nets in the dying embers in the fireplace; letters of the alphabet and pictures appeared, shapes recalling faces, animals, plants, worms and snakes. When I came to and looked at the man next to me, he was staring with fanatical devotion into the ashes, his chin on his fists.

"I have to go now," I said softly.

"All right, then go. See you later!"

He did not stand up, and since the lamp was out I had to feel my way laboriously through the dark room and down the dark hallways and staircases out of the enchanted old house. Out on the street I stopped and looked back up at it. Every window was dark. A little brass plaque gleamed in the light of the gas lamps by the door: "Pistorius, Head Vicar," I read.

Only when I sat down for dinner, alone in my little room, did I realize that I had learned nothing about either Abraxas or Pistorius, since we hadn't exchanged even a dozen words. Still, I was very happy with my visit to his house. And he had promised me a perfectly exquisite piece of old organ music for the next time I heard him play: a passacaglia by Buxtehude.

Without my realizing it, Pistorius the organist had given me his first lesson while I was lying on the floor with him in front of the fireplace in his gloomy hermit's room. Looking into the fire had been good for me; it had strengthened and confirmed certain inclinations I had always had but never actually carried out. Gradually I started to understand them better, at least in part.

Even as a small child I had often liked observing bizarre natural forms—not to study and analyze them, but to abandon myself to their unique magic, their confused, deep language. Long lignified tree roots, veins of color in rocks, patches of oil floating on water, cracks in glass: everything like that had cast a powerful spell on me back then, but especially water and fire, smoke, clouds, dust, and most of all the spinning spots of color I saw when I closed my eyes. In the days that followed my first visit to Pistorius's house, I started to remember these things again, and I realized that I felt a kind of joy and new strength, a heightened sense of myself, due simply to our long staring into the open flame. It was remarkably comforting and rewarding.

So now, joining the few experiences I had had until then on

the path to my life's true purpose, there was a new one. Contemplating such patterns, giving ourselves over to irrational, confused, bizarre natural forms, creates in us a feeling of harmony between our inner selves and the force that willed these patterns into being—before long we even feel tempted to see these patterns as our own moods, our own creations—we see the border between ourselves and nature quiver and melt away and learn what it feels like not to know whether the images on our retina come from external or internal impressions. Nowhere but in these practices can we so quickly and easily discover the extent to which we are creators, how greatly our own soul constantly participates in the continual creation of the world. Or rather it is the same indivisible divinity active in us and in nature, and if the external world were destroyed, any one of us would be able to rebuild it, for mountain and river, tree and leaf, root and blossom, every form in nature has its model and prototype within us and arises from the soul whose essence is eternity, whose nature we do not know but which shows itself primarily as the power to love and the power to create.

Only several years later did I find this observation confirmed in a book, by Leonardo da Vinci, who spoke of how good and deeply moving it is to look at a wall that many people have spit on. He felt the same, in front of those wet spots on the wall, as I felt in front of Pistorius's fire.

The next time we met, the organist explained: "We always draw the boundaries of our personal selves much too narrowly! We count as our selves only what we can distinguish as individual or anomalous. But really we are all made up of the substance of the whole world—every one of us. Just as our bodies carry inside them the whole genealogy of our evolution, back to fishes and much farther than that, so too our souls have everything the human soul has ever experienced inside them. All the gods and devils that ever existed, whether those of the Greeks or the Chinese, or the Zulu kaffirs, they are all inside us, all there as possibilities, as wishes, as outlets. If the whole human race died out except for one single halfway talented child who had never enjoyed any education, that child would rediscover the whole course of the world and could produce everything anew: gods, demons, paradises, commandments and prohibitions, the Old Testament and the New."

I objected: "Yes, all right, but then what is the individual worth? Why should we still strive for anything if we already have everything complete inside us?"

"Stop!" Pistorius cried violently. "There is a very big difference between having the world inside you and *knowing* it! An insane man can utter thoughts that recall Plato, a devout little Pietist schoolboy in a Herrnhut institute can reconstruct deep mythological connections found in Zoroaster or the Gnostics from his own creative spirit. But he doesn't know it! He is a tree, or a rock, or at most an animal, until he becomes conscious of it. Then, though, at the first glimmer of this consciousness: then he becomes human. You wouldn't call every biped you see on the street human, would you, just because they walk upright and carry their babies in the womb for nine months? You can see how many of them are fish or sheep, are worms or angels, how many are ants, how many are bees! Now every one of them contains the possibility of becoming human, but only when he intuits this possibility, or even learns to bring it at least partly into his consciousness, is it truly his."

Our conversations proceeded along these lines. They rarely surprised me, or gave me anything entirely new. But all of them, even the most ordinary, hit me in the same place with their soft, steady hammer blows; they all helped shape me, helped me shed my layers of skin, break the eggshell, and after every one I held my head up a little bit higher, with a little more freedom, until my yellow bird poked its gorgeous raptor's head out of the shattered shell of the world.

We also often told each other our dreams. Pistorius knew how to interpret them. One remarkable example comes back to me now: I had had a dream where I could fly, but only by building up momentum and being hurled through the air, as it were; I could not control my flight. It was a fine, noble feeling, but it soon turned frightening, as I saw myself hurtling up to a considerable height, powerless. Then I made the saving discovery that I could control my rising and falling by holding and releasing my breath.

Pistorius had this to say: "The force that hurls you into flight is the great treasure trove of our humanity, which we all possess. It is the feeling of connection with the roots of all power. But it gets scary in a hurry! It's damned dangerous! That's why most people are so happy to renounce flying. They'd rather stay safe on the sidewalk, following the rules. But not you. You keep flying, the way a brave fellow should. And look, then you discover the incredible thing: you can gradually get control of it. Along with the great universal power that hurls you through the sky, you have a delicate little power of your own, a bodily function, a way to steer. That's wonderful! People without it hurtle powerless through the sky—insane people, for example. Deeper intuitions have been given to them than to the law-abiding people on the sidewalks, but they have no key to them, no way to steer, so they plummet into the abyss. But you, Sinclair, you've got it! How? You probably don't even know, right? With a new organ, a breath regulator. Now you can see how little in the depths of your soul is 'personal.' You didn't invent this regulator, after all! It's nothing new! It's on loan to you; it has existed for thousands of years. It is the fish's air bladder, that it uses to keep its balance. And in fact, even today there are a few strange and primitive species of fish whose air bladders also function as a kind of lung—they can actually breathe air under certain circumstances. In other words, just like the lungs you used as a flight-bladder in your dream!"

He even brought me a zoology book and showed me the names and pictures of these antediluvian fish. And I felt, with a strange shudder, a bodily function from an early evolutionary period alive and well inside me.

CHAPTER SIX

JACOB WRESTLES
WITH THE ANGEL

I cannot summarize in brief what I learned about Abraxas from the strange musician, Pistorius. The most important thing I learned from him, though, was another step on the path to myself. I was an unusual young man then, around eighteen years old—precocious in a hundred ways but very far behind and helpless in a hundred other ways. When I compared myself to other people my age, as I would do every now and then, I sometimes felt proud and conceited but just as often demoralized and depressed. There were many times I saw myself as a genius, many times as half insane. I was never able to share and join in the others' pleasures, and I was eaten up with worries and self-hatred about how hopelessly isolated I was from them, how cut off from life.

Pistorius, an outsider himself, gave me courage and taught me to keep my self-respect. The way he always found something valuable in my words, my dreams, my thoughts and imaginings, always took them seriously and discussed them in earnest, became exemplary for me.

"You've told me you like music because it is outside of morality," he said. "Well and good. But now stop being a moralist yourself! You can't keep comparing yourself to other people—if nature has made you a bat, you can't decide you want to be an ostrich. You sometimes feel like you don't belong, you blame yourself for following a different path than most other people. You have to unlearn that. Stare into the fire, look at the clouds, and when ideas or intuitions come to you and the voices in your soul start to speak, trust them and don't worry about whether your teacher or your daddy or any other lord above likes what they have to say! That's what ruins a person. That's how you end up on the law-abiding sidewalk, just another fossil. My dear Sinclair, our god is called Abraxas, and he is God and Satan both, he contains the world of light and the world of darkness. Abraxas does not reject a single one of your thoughts and dreams. Never forget that. But he will leave you if you ever turn normal and irreproachable. Then he will leave you, and look for another pot to cook up his thoughts in."

Out of all my dreams, the dark sex dream was the most faithful. I dreamed it many, many times: stepping under the bird on the coat of arms into our old house, trying to take Mother in my arms and instead finding in my arms the large, half-masculine half-maternal woman I was afraid of and at the same time drawn to with the most desperate, burning desire. But I could never tell my friend about this dream. It was something I kept back even after I had revealed everything else to him. It was my private place, my secret, my refuge.

Whenever I felt depressed, I asked Pistorius if he would play me Buxtehude's passacaglia. I sat in the church in the evening darkness, lost in this strange, interior, self-absorbed music. It seemed to be listening to itself, and every time I heard it it helped me and made me more ready to heed my own inner voices.

Sometimes we stayed for a while, after the last notes of the organ faded away, and watched the weak light shine through the high windows with their pointed arches and disappear into the space of the church.

"It seems strange," Pistorius said, "that I used to be a divinity student and almost became a pastor. But it was just an error in form. It truly is my calling and my goal to be a priest. But I took the easy path and put myself at Jehovah's service before I knew Abraxas. Ah, every religion is beautiful. Religion is soul, irrespective of whether you take Christian communion or make the pilgrimage to Mecca."

"In that case," I said, "you could have gone ahead and become a pastor after all."

"No, Sinclair, no. I would have had to lie. Our religion is practiced as though it weren't a religion at all. It pretends to be a construction of reason. I could probably be Catholic if I had to, but a Protestant minister? No! The few true believers out there—I do know some—like to cling to literal meanings, I couldn't tell them that Christ for me is not a person but a mythical hero, a prodigious shadow picture in which humanity sees itself silhouetted on the wall of eternity. As for the others, the ones who come to church to hear a clever sermon, to do their duty, not miss anything, and so on—what could I say to them? Convert them, you think? But I don't want to, not at all! A priest doesn't want to convert anyone, he wants to live among the faithful, among people like him, and be the bearer and expression of the feeling out of which we make our gods."

He broke off. Then he continued: "Our new faith, for which we are choosing the name Abraxas, is a beautiful one, my friend. It is the best we have. But it is still in its infancy! It has not yet grown wings. A lonely religion, alas, is not yet the true one. It has to become communal, has to have rites and raptures, holidays and mysteries. . . ."

He sank into his own thoughts.

"Isn't it possible to celebrate mysteries alone, or in small groups?" I asked hesitantly.

"It's possible," he nodded. "I have done it myself, for a long time. I have performed rites that would land me in jail for years, if they knew. But I know that that is not yet the true way."

Suddenly he startled me by clapping me on the shoulder. "My boy," he said urgently, "you have mysteries too. I know that you must be having dreams you don't tell me about. I don't want to know what they are. But I tell you: Live your dreams! Act them out, build altars to them! It is not ideal, but it is a path. Time will tell whether or not we will renew the world—you and me and a few other people. But we have to renew it within ourselves, every day, otherwise we have nothing. Think about it! You're eighteen years old, Sinclair, you don't go with streetwalkers, you must have sex dreams, sexual urges. Maybe you're someone who's afraid of them. Don't be! They are the best things you have! Believe me. I lost a lot by strangling the sexual dreams I had when I was your age. You can't do that. Once you know about Abraxas, you mustn't. We cannot fear anything or treat anything our soul desires as forbidden."

I was shocked, and I objected: "But you can't just do anything you want! You can't kill someone just because you don't like him."

He moved closer to me.

"In certain circumstances, you can—that too. Only it's usually a mistake. And I'm not saying you should simply do whatever comes into your head. No, but these ideas have their own good sense, and you shouldn't make them harmful by repressing them and moralizing about them. Instead of nailing yourself or anyone else to the cross, you can drink wine from a chalice, think ceremonial thoughts, and consider the mystery of sacrifice that way. It is possible to treat your drives and so-called temptations with respect and love, even if you don't act on them. Then they show you what they mean—and they all do mean something. The next time something truly crazy or sinful occurs to you, Sinclair—when you want to kill someone or commit some other enormous horror—stop for a moment and think that this is Abraxas imagining within you! The person you want to kill isn't Mr. So-and-so: he is surely just a disguise. When we hate someone, what we hate is something in him, or in our image of him, that is part of ourselves. Nothing that isn't in us ever bothers us."

Nothing Pistorius ever said struck me so deeply, penetrating my innermost secrets. I couldn't respond. What affected me most powerfully and strangely, though, was the resonance between these words of encouragement and Demian's words I had carried inside me for so many years. They didn't know a thing about each other, and yet both of them had told me the same thing.

"The things we see," Pistorius said softly, "are the same things that are in us. There is no reality other than what we have inside us. That is why most people live such unreal lives, because they see external images as reality and never give their own internal world a chance to express itself. You can be

happy living like that, but once you know that there is another
way, you can no longer choose to follow the path of the many.
The path of the many is an easy one, Sinclair. Ours is hard. —
We are trying to follow it."

A few days later, after I had waited for him twice in vain, I
saw him on the street late at night. He came around the corner
as if blown by the cold night wind, alone, stumbling drunk. I
did not want to call his name. He walked past me without seeing me; he was staring straight ahead with burning, lonely
eyes, as though he were following a dark summons from the
unknown. I followed him down the street; he drifted along as
though pulled by an invisible string, with a fanatical and yet
exhausted gait, like a ghost. I sadly walked back home to my
own unrealized dreams.

"So *that's* how he renews the world inside him!" I thought,
and at the same moment I felt that this was a low and moralizing thing to think. What did I know of his dreams? Maybe
he was on a surer path in his drunkenness than I was in my
timidity.

I had started to notice, in the breaks between classes, that a
fellow student I had never paid attention to was trying to approach me. He was a short, skinny, weak-looking boy with
thin reddish-blond hair and something strange about how he
acted and the look in his eye. One evening when I was walking
home, he was loitering in the street waiting for me; he let me
pass, then ran after me and stopped in front of our front door
with me.

"Do you want something?" I asked.

"I just want to talk to you," he said shyly. "Please be so
good as to walk a little ways with me."

I followed him and could feel that he was deeply excited and
full of anticipation. His hands were shaking.

All of a sudden he asked: "Are you a spiritualist?"

"No, Knauer," I said with a laugh. "Not a bit. What makes
you think that?"

"But you're a theosophist, then?"

"No, not that either."

"Oh, don't be so secretive! I can see perfectly well that you're different somehow. It's in your eyes. I'm sure you communicate with spirits. . . . I'm not asking out of curiosity, Sinclair, no! I am a seeker too, you know, and I feel so alone."

"Tell me about it," I encouraged him. "I don't know anything about spirits, I just live in my dreams, that's what you noticed. Other people live in dreams too, but they're not their own dreams, that's the difference."

"Yes, you may be right," he whispered. "It all depends what kinds of dreams a person lives in. . . . Have you heard of white magic?"

I had to say no.

"That's where you learn self-mastery. You can become immortal, cast spells too. You've never practiced the exercises?"

I asked curious questions about these exercises, which made him cagey until I turned to walk away, then he dredged something up: "For example, when I want to fall asleep, or concentrate on something, I do one of these exercises. I think of something, a word or a name, a geometrical shape. Then I think it into myself as hard as I can. I try to see it inside my head, until I can feel it there, then I think it down into my neck, and so on, until it entirely fills me up. Then I am firmly grounded, and nothing can shake me."

I had a general sense of what he meant. Still I could tell he had something else on his mind. He was strangely excited and jittery. I tried to put him at ease, and before long he came out with what he actually wanted to say.

"You're abstinent too, aren't you? he asked anxiously.

"What do you mean? Sexually?"

"Yes, yes. I've been abstinent for two years now, ever since I first heard the teachings. Before then I committed a vice, you know. . . . So you've never been with a woman?"

"No," I said. "I haven't found the right one."

"But if you did find one you thought was right, you would sleep with her?"

"Yes, of course! If she didn't mind . . ." I said, a little mockingly.

"Oh, but that's a mistake! The only way to train your inner powers is to stay completely abstinent. I've stayed that way for two years. Two years and a little more than a month! It's so hard to do! Sometimes I think I can't stand it much longer."

"Listen, Knauer, I don't think abstinence is so terribly important."

"I know," he countered, "everyone says that. But I didn't expect it from you! Anyone trying to follow the higher spiritual path has to remain pure, absolutely!"

"All right, then do it! But I don't understand why someone who represses his sexuality is supposed to be 'purer' than anyone else. Can you keep sexuality out of all your thoughts and dreams too?"

He looked at me in despair.

"No, that's just it! Good God, and yet we have to. I have dreams at night that I can't even tell myself afterwards. Terrible dreams!"

I remembered what Pistorius had told me. But no matter how true I thought his words were, I could not relay them to someone else—I could not give advice that did not come from my own experience, advice that I myself didn't feel able to follow. I fell silent, humbled that someone was asking me for advice when I didn't have any to give.

"I've tried everything!" Knauer groaned, standing next to me. "I've done everything you can do—cold water, snow, exercise, running—but nothing helps. Every night I wake up from dreams that I can't bear to even think about. And the horrible thing is that I'm losing everything I've learned, spiritually. I can almost never do it anymore, concentrate on something or put myself to sleep. Sometimes I lie awake all night long. There's no way I can live like this for long. But if I finally have to throw in the towel, if I give up and make myself impure again, I'll be worse than all the others who never even tried. You understand that, don't you?"

I nodded but had nothing to say. The fact is, he was starting to bore me. Even though I was shocked at myself for not caring more deeply about his obvious pain and despair, all I felt was: I cannot help you.

"So, you have nothing to tell me?" he said at last, exhausted and miserable. "Nothing at all? There must be a way! How do you do it, then?"

"I have nothing to tell you, Knauer. No one can help anyone else. No one helped me either. You have to just reflect on yourself and then do what truly comes from your nature. There's nothing else. If you can't find yourself, then you won't find any spirits either, it seems to me."

The little fellow looked at me, disappointed and suddenly speechless. Then his eyes burned with sudden hate; he grimaced at me, furious, and screamed: "Oh you're a nice saint for me! You have your vices too, I know it! You act so wise and you secretly cling to the same filth as me and everyone else! You're a pig, a pig, like me. We are all pigs!"

I walked away and left him there. He took two or three steps after me, then stopped, turned around, and ran off. I felt queasy with pity and revulsion, and could not break free of the feeling until I got back to my little room, hung my couple pictures on the wall, and abandoned myself with the most fervent intensity to my own dreams. Right away my dream came back—of the door to the house and the coat of arms, my mother and the strange woman—and I saw the woman's features so clearly that I started to paint her picture that same night.

When, after a few days, the picture was finished—set down on paper almost unconsciously in dreamlike fifteen-minute bursts—I hung it on my wall, pulled the study lamp over to it, and stood before it as though it were a spirit I had to wrestle with until one of us won and the other one lost. It was a face like the earlier face; it was like my friend Demian's, and in some features like my own face too. One eye was noticeably higher than the other. The picture's gaze passed over me and was gone, in a glassy stare, full of destiny.

I stood there before it and felt a chill reaching deep into my chest from inner strain. I asked the image questions, I accused it, caressed it, prayed to it; I called it Mother, lover, whore, and slut, called it Abraxas. At some point Pistorius's words— or were they Demian's?—came to mind: I could not remember when I had heard them before, but felt that I was not hearing them for the first time. They were about Jacob wrestling with the angel of God, and his "I will not let thee go, except thou bless me."

The painted face in the lamplight was transformed every time I appealed to it. It was bright and shining, then black and dark; it closed wan lids over eyes that had died away into nothing, then opened them again so that burning looks flashed out. It was woman, man, girl—a young child, an animal, a blurry patch on the wall—and then big and clear again. Finally, obeying a powerful inner command, I closed my eyes and I saw the image within me, stronger and more powerful than ever. I wanted to kneel down before it, but it was so much a part of me that I could no longer distinguish it from myself. It was as though it had become entirely I.

Then I heard a dark, heavy roaring like that of a spring downpour, and I trembled with an indescribable new feeling of fear and experience. I saw stars flash and go out; memories reaching back to my earliest, most forgotten childhood and even farther, back to pre-existence and early stages of becoming, thronged past me, but these memories that seemed to repeat my whole life, down to its most hidden secrets, did not stop with yesterday, or today, they continued on, reflecting the future, tearing me away from the present into new forms of life. The images were immensely bright, almost blinding, but afterward I could not remember a single one, not the way they really were.

That night I woke up out of a very deep sleep, lying diagonally across the bed in my clothes. I turned on the light, felt that I had to remember something crucially important, but could not recall anything from the past few hours. I turned on the light, and gradually it came back to me. Then I looked for the picture, but it was not on the wall anymore—not on the table either. Then I thought I dimly recalled having burned it. Or was it a dream? That I had held it in my hands as it burned, and eaten the ashes?

Great spasms of anxiety drove me from my room. I put on my hat and hurried out of the house, down the street, as though under some kind of compulsion—through the streets, across the squares of the city, as though blown by a storm; I stopped and listened in the darkness in front of my friend's church; I searched and searched, driven by dark urges, not knowing what I was looking for. I passed through a part of the city where there were brothels, here and there with a light in the window. Farther out were building sites, piles of bricks partly covered with gray snow. As I passed like a sleepwalker roaming through a wasteland, compelled by a pressure from somewhere outside myself, I remembered the construction site at the edge of town where my tormentor, Kromer, had pulled me through the doorway and made me give him his first payment. There was a similar building here before me, the black hole of its door gaping open in the gray night. It drew me inside; I wanted to escape, and I dragged my feet in the sand and stumbled over the rubble, but the pull was too strong for me, I had to go in.

I stumbled over planks and broken bricks into the desolate room; there was a murky smell of stones and damp cold. A pile of sand, a light-gray patch, otherwise all was dark.

Then a horrified voice called out: "For God's sake, Sinclair, where did *you* come from?"

Next to me someone stood up out of the darkness: short and scrawny, like a phantom, and as the hairs stood up on the back of my neck I recognized my schoolmate Knauer.

"What made you come here?" he asked, half-insane with emotion. "How did you find me?"

I didn't understand.

"I wasn't looking for you," I said, dazed. It was difficult to talk; every word was an effort, struggling painfully out through my dead, heavy, almost frozen lips.

He stared at me.

"Not looking for me?"

"No. Something drew me here. Did you call me? You must have called me. What are you doing here anyway? It's the middle of the night!"

He frantically threw his thin arms around me.

"Yes, it's night, it must be almost dawn. Oh, Sinclair, you didn't forget me! Can you ever forgive me?"

"For what?"

"Oh, I was so beastly!"

Only then did I remember our conversation. It was, what, four or five days before? It seemed like a lifetime had passed since then. Then all at once I understood everything. Not only what had happened between us, but why I had come out here and what Knauer had been planning to do.

"You were going to kill yourself, weren't you, Knauer?"

He shivered with cold and fear.

"Yes, I wanted to. I don't know if I would have been able to. I was waiting until the sunrise."

I pulled him out into the open. The first horizontal rays of daylight, unspeakably cold and listless, gleamed in the gray air.

I led the boy by the arm a short way and heard a voice come out of my mouth: "Now go home and don't tell anyone about this! You've been on the wrong path, the wrong path! And we aren't pigs, like you said. We are human beings. We make gods and then wrestle with them, and they bless us."

We walked on and then parted, in silence. When I got home, it was day.

The best thing the rest of my time in St.— still had to offer was the hours I spent with Pistorius, listening to him play the organ or lying in front of his fireplace. We read a Greek text about Abraxas together; he read me passages from a translation of the Vedas and taught me how to utter the sacred "Om." And yet these scholarly matters weren't what encouraged my soul—rather the opposite. What did me good was my forging ahead inside myself, the growing trust I had in my own dreams, thoughts, and intuitions, and my increasing knowledge of the power I carried within me.

Pistorius and I understood each other in every way. I had only to think hard about him and I could be sure that he, or a message from him, would come to me from him. I could ask him something even if he wasn't there—like Demian: I just needed to picture him firmly in my mind and ask him my questions as concentrated thoughts, and all the power of my soul I put into the question came back to me as the answer. Only it wasn't the person of Pistorius that I imagined, nor that of Max Demian—instead I summoned up the image I had dreamed and painted, the male-female dream-image of my daemon. It was alive now, no longer only in my dreams or painted on paper, but in me, as an ideal, a heightening of my self.

The relationship that developed later between me and Knauer, the would-be suicide, was odd and sometimes even funny. Ever since the night I had been sent to save him, he clung to me like a faithful servant, or a dog, following me blindly and trying to join his life to mine. He came to me with the most bizarre questions and requests; he wanted to see spirits, wanted to study the kabbalah, and didn't believe me when I assured him I didn't know a thing about any of that. He thought I had every power imaginable. But the strange thing was, he often came to me with his bizarre and stupid questions just when there was some puzzle or another inside myself that I needed to solve, and his fanciful ideas and concerns often gave me the key push I needed to solve it. He was often a burden on me, and I would send him away in lordly fashion, but I nonetheless felt that he too was sent to me; even with him, what I gave returned to me twice as rich. He too was my guide, or even the path itself. The crazy books and tracts he brought me, in which he sought his salvation, taught me more than I realized at the time.

Later this Knauer fell away from my path, unnoticed. No confrontation with him was necessary. With Pistorius it was. Near the end of my time at school in St.—, I had one more strange experience with this friend.

Even the most harmless people can hardly avoid coming into conflict, once or twice in their lives, with the beautiful virtues of piety and gratitude. At some point we all have to take the step that separates us from our father and our teachers; we all have to feel something of the cruelty of solitude, even if most people cannot endure too much and quickly crawl back to safety.

I had not parted from my parents, from the "world of light"

of my wonderful childhood, in a violent struggle—I had slowly, almost imperceptibly, grown distant from it and more and more a stranger to it. I was sorry, I spent many bitter hours during my visits home, but it didn't touch me to the core, it was bearable.

But wherever we have given our love and respect not out of habit but out of our ownmost impulses—whenever we have been companions and friends with all our heart—it is a bitter and terrible moment when we suddenly recognize that the currents inside us are carrying us away from the one we once loved. When that happens, every thought pointing away from our friend or teacher is aimed like a poison arrow straight at our own heart—every defensive blow strikes us full in our own face. Then anyone who bears the reigning morality inside him feels the labels "betrayal" and "ingratitude" rise up like disgraceful, stigmatizing accusations; the terrified heart flees in fear, back to the lovely valleys of childhood virtues, and cannot bring itself to believe that this break too must be made, this connection too must be cut.

Slowly, over time, I started to feel myself turning against the idea that my friend Pistorius was my guide in all things. My friendship with him, his advice, his consolation, his closeness, had filled the most important months of my youth. God had spoken to me through him. My dreams had come back to me out of his mouth, clarified and interpreted. He had given me faith in myself. And now, alas! I felt my resistance against him slowly increasing. Too much of what he had to say was didactic; I felt that he fully understood only part of me.

There was no argument or scene between us, no break or day of reckoning. There was only one thing I said to him, actually quite harmless—and yet that was the moment when an illusion between us shattered into brightly colored shards.

I had felt the intuition weighing down on me for some time, and it became a clear feeling one Sunday in his old study. We were lying in front of the fire and he was telling me about mysteries and the other religious forms he studied and longed for, whose possibilities for the future he spent his time brooding over. To me, though, it was all curious and interesting rather than vitally important—I could hear a note of mere pedantry in his words, an exhausted rummaging around under the rubble of bygone worlds. And suddenly I felt revulsion against everything about it: this cult of mythologies, this game of making mosaics out of the forms of belief from the past.

"Pistorius," I said all of a sudden, in a burst of malice that shocked and surprised me myself, "you should tell me one of your dreams again—I mean a real dream, the kind you have at night. What you're saying now is so—so damned antiquarian!"

He had never heard me talk like that, and I myself felt, at that very moment—in a lightning flash of shame and horror—that the arrow I had just shot, which had struck him right in the heart, had been drawn from his own arsenal. I had taken self-criticisms I had sometimes heard him express ironically, and wickedly shot them back at him, sharper than before.

He felt it at once and immediately fell silent. I looked at him with fear in my heart and saw him turn terribly pale.

After a long, painful pause, he put another log on the fire and said quietly: "You are absolutely right, Sinclair. You're a smart one. I'll spare you any more antiquarianism."

He spoke very calmly, but I could easily hear the wounded pain in what he said. What had I done?

I was almost in tears. I wanted to give him a kind look, ask his forgiveness, swear my love and gratitude. Soothing words came to mind . . . but I couldn't speak them. I lay there, looked into the fire, and said nothing. He was silent too. So we lay there, and the fire dwindled and died down, and with every fading tongue of flame I felt something sincere and beautiful smolder and vanish, never to return.

"I'm afraid you misunderstood me," I finally said, under great strain and with a dry, hoarse voice. These stupid, meaningless words came to my lips almost mechanically, as though I were reading them out of a pulp novel.

"I understood you perfectly," Pistorius said softly. "You are absolutely right." He waited. Then he slowly went on: "Insofar as anyone can be in the right against someone."

No, no! I heard the cry inside me, I'm wrong!—but I couldn't say anything. I knew that my one simple word had found an essential weakness, a wound, a need in him. I had touched the sore spot where he did not trust himself. His ideal *was* "antiquarian"—he was a seeker in the past, a Romantic. And all at once I felt, deep inside me: what Pistorius had been to me, and given me, was exactly what he could not be and give to himself. He had led me along a path that would run past and leave behind even him, the guide.

God knows where these things we say come from! I wasn't trying to be nasty, and had no idea of the disaster my comment would cause. I had said something I didn't understand at all when I said it; I had indulged in the impulse of a moment, a little bit clever and a little bit mean, and it had turned out to be fate. My careless minor act of cruelty was for him a judgment.

Oh, how I wanted him to get angry, defend himself, scream at me! He did none of that, so I had to do it all myself, on the inside. He would have smiled, if he could have. The fact that he couldn't showed more clearly than anything else how badly I had hurt him.

Pistorius, by so calmly accepting this blow from me, his insolent and ungrateful pupil—by saying nothing, by accepting that I was right, by taking my word as law and fate—made me hate myself, and made my impetuous remark a thousand times worse. When I'd lashed out I thought it was at someone sturdy and strong—and now he had turned into a meek, quiet, suffering little man, defenseless and acquiescing without a word.

We stayed in front of the dying fire a long time. Every glowing shape in it, every crumbling log of ash, reminded me of happy, rich, and beautiful hours and piled up what I owed to Pistorius higher and higher. Eventually I couldn't take it anymore. I stood up and left. I lingered at his door for a long time, on the dark stairs for a long time, waited outside the house for a long time to see if perhaps he would come and follow me. Then I walked away, wandered through the city and its outskirts, the park and the forest for hours and hours, until night fell. That was when, for the first time, I felt the mark of Cain on my forehead.

Only gradually was I able to think clearly about what had

happened. My thoughts were all meant to accuse myself and defend Pistorius, but they all ended up doing precisely the opposite. I was ready to repent and take back my rash words, a thousand times over—and yet the fact was that they were true. Only now did I fully understand Pistorius, only now could I put together the whole structure of his dream. He had wanted to be a priest, proclaim the new religion, institute new forms of exaltation, love, and worship, and create new symbols. But this was not his strength, and not his task. He was only too happy to linger in the past—he knew all too much about what had come before: Egypt, India, Mithras, Abraxas. His love was tied to images the world had already seen, even while he knew deep down that the new would be different and *new,* that it would spring up from fresh soil and not need to be cobbled together out of libraries and museums. Perhaps his true task was to help lead people to themselves, the way he had me. His task was not, in fact, to give them that tremendous thing, the new gods.

At this point the realization suddenly flared within me like a sharp burst of flame: everyone has his "task," but it is never a task he can choose for himself, can define and carry out however he wants. It was wrong to want new gods, it was utterly wrong to want to give the world anything! For awakened human beings, there was no obligation—none, none, none at all—except this: to search for yourself, become sure of yourself, feel your way forward along your own path, wherever it led. — This realization upset me deeply, and that was what I gained from the whole experience. I had often toyed with ideas and images of my future, dreaming up roles to play: as a writer, for example, or prophet, or painter, or whatever it was. All that meant nothing. I was not put on earth to write, or preach, or paint—and nor was anyone else. These things were only secondary. Every person's true calling was only to arrive at himself. He might end up a poet or a madman, a prophet or a criminal—that was no concern of his; in the end it was meaningless. His concern was to find his own fate, not a random one, and to live it out, full and complete. Everything else was a half-measure, escapism, fleeing back into the ideal of the masses—conformity and fear of what was inside yourself.

This new picture rose up before my eyes, terrifying and sacred, foreshadowed and suspected a hundred times, maybe even spoken out loud many times, and yet only now truly experienced. I was a roll of Nature's dice, thrown into the unknown, maybe into a new world, maybe into the void, and my only purpose in life was to let this throw from the primal depths play out, feel its will inside me, and make that will entirely my own. Only that!

I had already tasted great loneliness. Now I began to suspect the existence of even deeper solitudes, and that they were inescapable.

I made no effort to reconcile with Pistorius. We stayed friends, but our relationship had changed. We spoke about it only once, or actually only he did. He said: "I want to become a priest, as you know. I wanted most of all to become a priest of the new religion we have all these intuitions about. But I'll never be able to—I know that. I've known it for a long time, without ever entirely admitting it to myself. There are other priestly duties for me to perform, maybe on the organ, maybe some other way. But I need to feel beautiful and holy things around me, always: music, mystery cults, symbols, myths. I need it, and I refuse to give it up. . . . That's my fatal flaw. I know it, Sinclair—every now and then I know that I shouldn't have such desires, they are a luxury, a weakness. It would be better to put myself at the mercy of fate without making any demands. Truer too. But I can't do it. It's the one thing I can't do. Maybe you will be able to do it someday. It's hard—it's the only truly difficult thing there is, my boy. I have often dreamed of doing it, but I can't, I tremble at the thought of it. I cannot stand so utterly naked and alone, I'm like all the rest, a poor weak dog who needs warmth and food, and sometimes needs to feel close to others of his own kind. If you really and truly want nothing except your fate, there no longer *is* anyone of your own kind, you're completely alone with only the cold universe around you. That is Jesus in the garden of Gethsemane, you understand. There have been martyrs who were happy to let themselves be nailed to the cross, but they weren't heroes either, they weren't free: they too clung to what was familiar and comfortable for them, they followed others' examples, they had ideals. Anyone who wants nothing but fate has no model, no ideal, nothing he cares about, no consolation left! And that is the path we actually should follow. People like us are very lonely, but at least we have each other, and the secret satisfaction of being different, of rebelling, of wanting something out of the ordinary. That has to fall away too if you want to follow your path to the end. You can't want to be a revolutionary either, or an example to others, or a martyr. It's inconceivable. . . ."

Yes, it was inconceivable. But it could be dreamed, approached, intuited. I felt something of it myself a few times, when I found myself in moments of absolute stillness. Then I peered into myself and looked the image of my destiny right in its open, staring eyes. Those eyes might be full of wisdom or full of madness, might shine with love or evil, it was all the same to me. It was impossible to choose, impermissible to want anything about it. You must want only *yourself,* your own fate. Pistorius had guided me a good way toward it.

I wandered around as if blind in those days, with a storm raging inside me. Every step was dangerous. I saw nothing but a dark abyss before me—every path I had known led into and vanished into its depths. And in my soul I saw the image of my guide, who looked like Demian and whose eyes held my fate.

I wrote on a sheet of paper: "A guide has left me. I am in total darkness. I cannot take a single step alone. Help me!"

I wanted to send it to Demian. And yet I refrained; every time I wanted to do it, it seemed silly and pointless. Still, I knew this little prayer by heart and often said it to myself. It was with me every hour of the day and night. I began to have a sense of what prayer is.

My schooldays were over. I was supposed to take a trip during vacation—my father had planned it—and then enroll in the university. I did not know which field. A semester in the philosophy department was approved, but I would have been just as happy with any other.

CHAPTER SEVEN

EVE

One time, over vacation, I went by the house where Max Demian had lived with his mother, years before. An old woman was strolling in the garden; I talked to her and learned the house was hers. I asked after the Demian family. She remembered them well. But she didn't know where they were living now. She could tell I was interested, so she took me into the house, dug up a leather photo album, and showed me a picture of Demian's mother. I could barely remember her, but when I saw the little portrait, my heart stood still. — It was the picture from my dream! It was her: the large, almost masculine figure, resembling her son; the signs of maternal love, strictness, and deep passion in her features; beautiful and enticing, beautiful and unapproachable, daemon and mother, fate and lover. It was her!

What a wild miracle that was for me, to learn that my dream-image was alive in the world! There was a woman who actually looked like that—who bore the features of my destiny! Where was she? Where? — And she was Demian's mother.

Not long afterward I went away on my trip. What a strange trip it was! I traveled restlessly from place to place, following every impulse that came to me, in search of this woman. There were days when I saw nothing but figures who reminded me of her, echoed her, resembled her—who lured me down the streets of foreign cities, through train stations, into train cars, as in a long, confused dream. There were other days when I realized how useless my search was; then I sat in some park or other, in a hotel garden, in a waiting room, doing nothing, peering into myself and trying to bring the image in me to life.

But it had turned shy and fugitive. I was never able to fall asleep—at most I nodded off for fifteen minutes during train rides through unfamiliar landscapes. One time, in Zurich, a woman followed me. She was pretty, and quite brazen, but I barely noticed her and kept walking as though she were thin air. I would rather have died than take an interest in any other woman for even an hour.

I felt my destiny drawing me on—I felt that fulfillment was near, and I was insanely impatient and frustrated not to be able to bring it about. Once, at a train station in Innsbruck I think it was, I saw a shape through the window of a departing train that reminded me of her, and I was miserable for days. Suddenly the shape appeared to me again at night, in a dream, and I woke up feeling ashamed and empty, convinced of the senselessness of my hunt. I took the next train straight home.

A few weeks later I enrolled at the University of H—. Everything was a disappointment to me. The lectures I heard on the history of philosophy were as trivial and mass-produced as the hustle and bustle of the young students. Everything followed the same clichéd pattern, everyone did the same things as everyone else, and the good cheer on the flushed, boyish faces looked so depressingly empty and prefabricated! I was free, though; I had all my time to myself, and I lived in a nice, quiet, run-down place by the city walls with a couple volumes of Nietzsche on my table. I lived with him, felt the loneliness of his soul, trembled at the fate that had inexorably hounded him, suffered with him, and was overjoyed that there had been someone who had followed his path so relentlessly.

Late one night I wandered through the city, in gusts of autumn wind, and heard groups of students singing in the bars. Clouds of tobacco smoke poured out through the open windows, and torrents of song, loud and strictly rhythmical but utterly lifeless, joyless, and mechanical.

I stood on a street corner and listened. Right on schedule, the students' well-rehearsed high spirits echoed out into the night. Everywhere a communal huddling together, young men unburdening themselves of fate, fleeing to the warmth of the herd!

Two men slowly walked by, behind me, and I heard a snatch of their conversation.

"Isn't it exactly like the young men's house in an African village?" one of them said. "Everything is the way it's supposed to be, down to the prescribed tattoos of their dueling scars! Here you have it: the future of Europe."

The voice somehow reminded me of something—I knew that voice. I followed the men down the dark street. One of them was Japanese, a small, elegant man; I could see his yellow face light up in a smile under a streetlamp.

Then the other man spoke again.

"Well I'm sure it's no better with you in Japan. It is always rare to find people who don't follow the herd. Even here there are some."

I felt a stab of joyous shock with every word. I knew the person who was speaking—it was Demian.

I followed him and the Japanese man through the windy night, down dark streets; I listened to their conversation and was happy to hear the sound of Demian's voice. It had the same old tone from before, the same beautiful confidence and serenity, the same power over me. Now everything was going to be all right. I had found him.

At the end of a street on the edge of the city, the Japanese man said goodbye and opened his front door. Demian started to walk back; I had stopped and was waiting for him in the middle of the street. With my heart pounding I saw him walk toward me, standing up straight, a spring in his step, wearing a brown plastic raincoat and with a thin cane hanging on his arm. Without altering his stride he walked right up to me, took off his hat, and revealed the same old bright face with its decisive mouth and strangely bright forehead.

"Demian!" I cried.

He held out his hand to me.

"There you are, Sinclair! I've been expecting you."

"You knew I was here?"

"I wasn't sure, but I was definitely hoping. I hadn't seen you until tonight. You've been following us."

"So you recognized me right away?"

"Of course. It's true, you've changed. But you have the sign."

"The sign? What sign?"

"We used to call it the mark of Cain, if you recall. It is our special sign. You always had it—that's why I wanted to be your friend. But now it's clearer."

"I didn't know. Or, actually, I did. I painted a picture of you once, Demian, and I was amazed to see that it also looked like me. Was that the sign?"

"It was. It's good that you're here! My mother will be glad too."

I was suddenly frightened. "Your mother? Is she here? She doesn't even know me."

"Oh, she knows about you. She will know who you are even if I don't tell her. . . . You haven't been in touch for a long time."

"Oh, I wanted to write to you, so many times, but I couldn't. I've felt for a while that I'd find you soon. I waited for it every day."

He tucked his arm into mine and walked on with me, exuding a calm that entered me too. Soon we were chatting the same way we used to. We recalled our school days, the confirmation class, and the meeting that hadn't gone well during the school break too—the only thing we didn't discuss was the earliest, closest bond between us, the Franz Kromer story.

We unexpectedly found ourselves in the middle of a strange conversation, full of premonitions and forebodings. We had just been discussing student life, along the lines of Demian's conversation with the Japanese man, and had moved on from that to other things that seemed to be totally unrelated, but Demian's words revealed an underlying connection.

He spoke of the spirit of Europe, and the nature of our age. Everywhere, he said, conformity and the herd instinct prevail; nowhere do freedom and love have the upper hand. All this gathering together, from student fraternities and singing clubs to entire nations, is taking place under a kind of compulsion— they are communities of anxiety, fear, and shame, and on the inside they are old and rotten and about to collapse.

"Community is a beautiful thing," Demian said. "But what we see flourishing everywhere around us is no such thing. True community will arise again when actual individuals come to know each other; then will come a time when it reshapes the world. The communities we have now are just herds. People run as fast as they can to each other because they're afraid of each other—the rich come together over here, the workers over there, the educated elites somewhere else! And why are they afraid? Fear always comes from a split in yourself. They are afraid because they have never gotten to know who they really are. A whole society of people afraid of the unknown in their own hearts! They all can feel that the principles they live by are not valid anymore, that they're following the old laws; none of it, neither their religion nor their morality, is right for us today. For a hundred years and more, Europe has done nothing but go to school and build factories! They know exactly how many ounces of powder it takes to kill someone, but don't know how to pray to God. They don't even know how to be happy for an hour at a time. Just look at these student bars! Or anywhere rich people go to amuse themselves! It's hopeless!

"My dear Sinclair, nothing good can come of all this. These people huddling together so timidly are full of fear and full of wickedness; no one trusts the next. They cling to ideals that no longer exist, and throw stones at anyone who is trying to create a new one. I can feel the conflicts. They will come, believe me, and soon! And naturally they won't make the world 'better.' Whether the workers kill their capitalists or Russia and Germany blow each other to bits, the only thing that'll change is who owns whom. But still it won't have been in vain. These conflicts will clarify how worthless the current ideals have become; they will wipe out all our old stone age gods. The world as it is wants to die, it cries out to be destroyed—and it will be."

"And what about us?" I asked.

"Us? Oh, maybe we will be destroyed too. Our kind can be shot and killed too. But they can't get rid of us that easily. The will of the future will collect around whatever remains of us, or whichever ones of us survive. The will of humanity, which

our European marketplace of science and technology has
strangled for so long, will reveal itself. And then it will be as
clear as day that the will of humanity has nothing, nothing to
do with the so-called communities we have today—the nations and tribes, the clubs and churches. What Nature wants
with us human beings always stands written in individuals: in
you and in me. It was there in Jesus, it was there in Nietzsche.
Those are the only tendencies that matter—of course their ap-
pearance may change day to day—and there will be room for
them once today's collectivities collapse."

It was late when we arrived at a garden by a river, and
stopped.

"This is where we live," Demian said. "Come see us soon.
We're waiting for you."

I happily walked the long road home. The night had grown
cool; here and there a student staggered noisily through the
city to wherever he was going. I had often thought how op-
posed their ridiculous high spirits were to my lonely life—
sometimes feeling I was missing out on something, sometimes
simply looking down on them. But I had never felt so calm, so
filled with secret strength, as I did that night. How little that
world had to do with me, how distant and forgotten it was! I
remembered civil servants from my hometown: dignified old
gentlemen who clung to the memories of their drunken student nights like souvenirs from a blissful paradise, and who
worshipped at the altar of the long-vanished "freedom" of
their student years the way poets or other Romantics did with
childhood. It was the same everywhere! Everywhere they
sought "freedom" and "happiness" somewhere behind them,
purely out of fear that they might be reminded of their responsibility for their own lives, might be admonished to follow
their own path. A few years of boozing and carousing, then
they knuckled under and turned into respectable bureaucrats.
Yes, it was rotten here, putrid, and these student idiocies were
not as bad or as idiotic as a hundred others.

In any case, by the time I got back to my distant apartment
and went to bed, all these thoughts had vanished, and my
whole soul clung expectantly to the great promise that had

been made to me. Whenever I wanted to—tomorrow, even—I would see Demian's mother. Let the students go on their drinking binges and scar one another's faces, let the rotten world await its own destruction—what did I care? The only thing I awaited was the encounter with my destiny in a new form, a new image.

I slept deeply until late the next morning. The new day dawned for me as a glorious holiday, of a kind I had not had since the Christmas celebrations of my childhood. I was full of inner restlessness but without a hint of fear. I felt that an important day in my life had arrived; the world around me seemed transformed, solemnly and meaningfully waiting; even the soft, flowing autumn rain was beautiful: silently, ceremoniously full of serious yet joyful music. It was the first time the outside world was in pure harmony with my inner world, and that is a high holiday of the soul—a day that makes it worthwhile to be alive. Not a single building or shop window or face on the street bothered me; everything was as it should be, and yet it did not wear the empty face of the habitual and everyday. Instead nature was waiting, standing worshipfully ready to meet its destiny. That was how I had seen the world as a boy, on the mornings of the important holidays, Christmas and Easter. I hadn't realized this world could still be so beautiful. I had gotten used to my inward-facing life, and had come to terms with the fact that the life out there had lost all meaning for me; I had decided that losing the glittering colors of the world inevitably went along with the loss of childhood, and that to a certain extent you had to pay for the freedom and manhood of the soul by renouncing that beloved shimmer. Now, enchanted, I saw that it had all merely been overshadowed and covered up, and that it was possible, even as a free man who had renounced childhood happiness, to see the world aglow and feel the heartfelt quiver of childlike vision.

The moment came when I found the garden on the edge of town once more, where I had parted from Demian the night before. Hidden behind tall, rain-gray trees was a small house, bright and homey, with large flowering plants behind a big glass pane, and clear, shining windows revealing dark walls with pictures and bookshelves. The front door led straight into a small heated hallway, and a silent old maid, in black with a white apron, showed me in and took my coat.

She left me alone in the hall. I looked around, and right away I was in the middle of my dream. High up on the dark wooden wall, above a door, hung a black frame, and under the glass was a picture I knew well: my bird with the golden yellow sparrow hawk head, vaulting out of the world-egg. I stood there, deeply moved—I had so much joy and sorrow in my heart, as though everything I had ever done and ever felt was coming back to me in that moment, as answer, as fulfillment. I saw image after image streak like lightning across my soul: my father's house back home, with the old stone coat of arms above the arch of the gate; Demian as a young man drawing the coat of arms; myself as a scared boy trapped in the evil clutches of my enemy, Kromer; myself as a teenager, sitting at the quiet table in my little student room and painting the bird of my yearnings, my soul tangled up in the net of its own threads—and everything, everything down to that moment echoed inside me, having been answered at last with affirmation and approval.

With tears in my eyes I stared at my picture and read myself. Then I looked farther down, and there, in the open door, under the picture of the bird, stood a tall woman in a black dress. It was her.

I couldn't speak a word. With a face timeless and ageless and imbued with will, like her son's, the beautiful, sacred woman gave me a friendly smile. Her gaze was fulfillment, her greeting meant I had come home. I silently held out my hand to her, and she took it in both of her firm, warm hands.

"You must be Sinclair. I recognized you right away. Welcome!"

Her voice was deep and warm, and I drank it in like sweet wine. Then I looked up, into her quiet face, into her black, unfathomable eyes, at her lively, ripe mouth, and at her free and imperious brow, which bore the sign.

"How happy I am!" I said to her, and I kissed her hands. "I

feel like I have been on a journey my whole life—and now I've come home."

She smiled a maternal smile.

"No one can ever go home," came her friendly reply. "But when friends' paths meet, the whole world can look like home for a time."

Her words expressed what I had been feeling on my way to her. Her voice as well as her words were very like her son's, and yet completely different. Everything was more mature and warmer, more direct. But the same way Max, long ago, had never seemed like a boy, his mother did not come across in the least like the mother of a grown son: her face and hair smelled so young and sweet, her golden skin was so taut and smooth, her mouth so radiant. She stood before me even more regal than she had been in my dream, and to be this close to her was to feel the joy of love. Her gaze was fulfillment.

So this was the new form in which my fate revealed itself to me: no longer stern and isolating but ripe and joyful! I came to no decisions at that moment, I took no vows—I had arrived, at a goal, a high point of the path, from which I could see the way ahead, long and majestic, reaching into promised lands, shaded by treetops of nearby happiness, cooled by nearby gardens of every pleasure. Whatever might happen to me now, I had been blessed with the knowledge that this woman was in the world, and was ecstatic to be able to drink in her voice and breathe in her closeness. Whether she be a mother to me, or a lover, or a goddess—as long as she was there, as long as my path ran next to hers!

She pointed up at my hawk picture.

"You never made our Max happier than with that picture," she said pensively. "And me as well. We were waiting for you, and when the picture came we knew you were on the way to us. When you were a little boy, Sinclair, my son came home from school one day and said: There's a boy there with the mark on his forehead, I have to make him my friend. It was you. You did not have it easy, but we had faith in you. One time, when you were home for the holidays, you met up with

Max. You must have been around sixteen years old. Max told me about it. . . ."

I interrupted her. "Oh, he told you? That was the most miserable time of my life!"

"Yes. Max told me that Sinclair has the hardest part ahead of him: he is trying to flee back into a community, he's hanging around bars. But he won't be able to do it. His mark is obscured, but secretly it is burning him. — Isn't that how it was?"

"Yes, exactly. Then I found Beatrice, and then, at last, another guide came to me. His name was Pistorius. Only then did I realize why my childhood was so closely tied to Max, why I couldn't get free of him. Dear Lady—dear Mother—back then I often thought I would have to take my own life. Is the path that hard for everyone?"

She ran her hand over my hair, as soft as a gentle breeze.

"It is always hard to be born. You know it—the bird has to struggle to get out of the egg. Think back and ask yourself: Was the path really so hard? Was it only hard? Wasn't it lovely too? Do you wish you had had a prettier, easier way?"

I shook my head.

"It was hard," I said, as though asleep, "it was hard until the dream came."

She nodded and gave me a piercing look.

"Yes, we all have to find our dream, then the path becomes easy. But no dream lasts forever. Every dream is supplanted by a new one, and you can't try to hold tight to any of them."

I was suddenly frightened. Was that a warning? Was it rejection, already? But whatever it was I was ready to let her be my guide and not ask where she was leading me.

"I don't know how long my dream will last," I said. "I hope it's forever. Under the picture of the bird my destiny has welcomed me, like a mother and like a lover. I belong to that destiny and to no one else."

"For as long as that dream is your destiny, you should stay true to it," she affirmed in a serious voice.

I was gripped with sadness and the desperate desire to die in this enchanted hour. I felt tears well up inside me and overpower me, irresistibly—it had been so infinitely long since the last time I'd cried! I turned violently away from her, stepped over to the window, and looked out past the flowerpots with blind eyes.

Behind me I heard her voice. It sounded calm, and nonetheless as full of affection as a goblet filled to the rim with wine.

"Sinclair, you're acting like a child! Your destiny loves you. It will be completely yours someday, just how you dream it, as long as you stay true to it."

I had regained control of myself and I turned back to face her again. She gave me her hand.

"I have a few friends," she said with a smile, "a few—very few, very close—friends who call me Eve. You can use my first name too, if you want."

She led me to the door, opened it, and pointed out into the garden. "You'll find Max out there."

I stood under the tall trees, numb and shaken, either wider awake or more deeply dreaming than ever, I wasn't sure. The rain dripped gently from the branches. I walked slowly into the garden, which extended a long way up and down the riverbank. Finally I found Demian. He was in an open summer house, shirtless, practicing boxing with a hanging sandbag.

I stood rooted to the spot. Demian looked magnificent, with his broad chest, firm, manly head, and raised arms with huge, taut, strong muscles. Movements burst from his hips, shoulders, and wrists like playing fountains.

"Demian!" I called out. "What are you doing there?"

He gave a cheerful laugh.

"Training. I've promised my little Japanese friend a match, and he's quick as a cat and just as spiteful. But he won't beat me. There's a tiny little humiliation I need to pay him back for."

He pulled on a shirt and jacket.

"You've already been to see my mother?" he asked.

"Yes, Demian, what a glorious mother you have! And: Eve! The name fits her perfectly, she really is like the mother of us all."

He looked thoughtfully into my face for a moment.

"She's already told you her first name? You can be proud, my boy, you are the first person she's ever told it to the first time she met him."

From that day on I came and went in their house like a son and a brother, although also like a lover. As soon as I had shut the gates behind me—actually as soon as I'd seen, from a distance, the tops of the garden's tall trees—I was rich, I was happy. Outside was "reality"; outside were streets and buildings, people and institutions, libraries and lecture halls—but here inside was light, and the soul; here dreams and fairy tales had come to life. And yet we did not live cut off from the world at all—in our thoughts and our conversations we were usually right in the middle of it, only on a different plane. It was not borders and frontiers that separated us from the mass of men, but rather a different way of seeing. Our task was to play the role of an island in the world—maybe we would be a model for others, maybe not, but either way we would proclaim that there were other possible ways to live. I, who had been lonely for so long, learned what true community means, the kind that is possible between people who have felt complete and total solitude. Never again did I yearn for the tables of the happy or the feasts of the blessed; never again did envy or longing for the past come over me at the sight of groups of people. I was slowly being initiated into the mystery of those who bore "the mark."

We, with the mark, might justly be considered strange, even crazy and dangerous, by the rest of the world. We were awakened, or at least awakening; our efforts were directed toward ever more complete awareness, while others always longed to merge their opinions, ideals, and duties, their lives and their happiness, more and more closely with those of the herd. That was a striving too—there was strength in that effort, and even a kind of greatness. But we, with the sign, felt that we embodied nature's will for the new, the individual, and the future, while the others' lives showed only a will to persist in the old. They loved humanity as much as we did, but for them it was something already finished, to be preserved and protected, while for us it lay in a distant future we were all moving toward, whose image was still unknown, and whose laws had never been written.

Aside from Eve, Max, and me, other seekers of very different kinds belonged to our circle, more or less intimately. Some of them followed strange paths, devoted themselves to bizarre goals, and clung to opinions and practices far outside the mainstream. The group included astrologers and kabbalists, a follower of Count Tolstoy, and all sorts of fragile, shy, and vulnerable types—followers of new sects, devotees of yoga, vegetarians, and others. In fact we had nothing in common with them spiritually, except for the mutual respect everyone showed for one another's esoteric ideals. We felt closer to other members of the group, the ones who pursued mankind's search for gods and new ideals in the past. Their studies often reminded me of those of my old friend Pistorius. They brought books with them, translated texts from ancient languages for us, showed us reproductions of old symbols and depictions of ancient rites, and taught us to see how every ideal the human race had ever possessed was a dream from the unconscious soul, dreams in which mankind had gropingly followed the dim premonitions of its future possibilities. And so we ran through the wondrous, thousand-headed chaos of gods from the ancient world, all the way up to the conversion to Christianity; we learned about the beliefs of the solitary saints and the changes and transformations that religions underwent from one people to the next. Everything we collected led us to the same critique of our time and the Europe of our day: its titanic endeavors had created powerful new human weapons but had finally ended in a profound and scandalous desolation of spirit. It had conquered the whole world only to lose its own soul.

Our group also included believers and adherents of various doctrines of salvation. There were Buddhists who wanted to convert Europe, Tolstoyans, and other faiths too. We in the inner circle listened to them but took none of their teachings as anything but a symbol. We who bore the sign felt no concern whatsoever for how the future would look. Every faith, every doctrine of salvation, seemed equally dead and useless to us from the start. We recognized only one thing as our duty and destiny: every one of us had to become himself, had to be true to and live for the sake of the seed of nature at work in himself, so completely that the uncertain future would find us ready for anything and everything it might bring.

For it was equally clear to us all, whether the sense was spoken or unspoken, that a new birth and the collapse of the present world were near, and already discernible. Demian sometimes told me: "No one can imagine what will come. Europe's soul is an animal that has lain in chains for an eternity. When it is free at last, its first stirrings will not be the sweetest and gentlest. But how we get there doesn't matter, as long as the true needs of the soul—so anesthetized and buried with lies for so long—see the light of day at last. Then our day will have come. They will need us, not as a guide or a giver of new laws (we will not live to see the new laws) but as the ones who are ready and willing to go and stand wherever destiny summons us. Look, anyone is prepared to do incredible things when his ideals are threatened, but when a new ideal, a new and perhaps dangerous or sinister stirring of growth comes knocking, there is no one. The few who will stand up and join in the transformation—will be us. That is what we are marked for, the same way Cain was marked to arouse fear and hate and to drive the humanity that existed then out of its cramped idyll into the wide, dangerous world. Everyone who has changed the course of human history, every last one was able to do so only because he was ready for his destiny. That's true of Moses and the Buddha, Napoleon and Bismarck. The wave that carries us, the star that guides us—we cannot choose it. If Bismarck had sympathized with the Social Democrats and joined them, he would have been an intelligent man but not a man of destiny. The same with Napoleon, with Caesar, with Ignatius of Loyola, with everyone! You have to think of these things in biological, evolutionary terms, always! When radical changes on the earth's surface hurled sea creatures onto dry land, or land animals back into the water, the specimens ready for their destiny were the ones that carried out the new, unimaginable transformation and adapted to save their species.

Maybe up until then these specimens had stood out among their kind as conservative preservers of the past, or maybe they were the outsiders and revolutionaries, we don't know. But they were ready, and so they could save their species by evolving into something new. That we know. That is what we are ready for too."

Eve was often present during conversations like this, but she didn't talk the same way. All of us who expressed our thoughts found a listener in her, an echo, full of trust and understanding. It seemed as though all the thoughts originated with her and were only returning back to her. Sitting near her, hearing her voice now, and breathing in the atmosphere of soulful maturity that surrounded her—that was what made me happy.

She sensed at once when any change took place in me: any dullness of spirit or any renewal. The dreams I had in my sleep seemed to me to have been sent by her. I often told her about them, and she always found them comprehensible and natural; there were no details her sensitive feelings could not follow. For a time I had dreams that were like replicas of our daytime conversations: I dreamed that the whole world was in turmoil and that I, either alone or with Demian, was waiting anxiously for the great destiny to come. It stayed hidden, but somehow it bore Eve's features. To be chosen by her or rejected by her was what destiny meant.

Sometimes she said with a smile: "That's not your whole dream, Sinclair, you've forgotten the best part"—and then it sometimes happened that another part of the dream came back to me, and I couldn't understand how I could possibly have forgotten it.

At times, all this wasn't enough; I was tortured with desire. I thought I could not bear seeing her next to me without taking her in my arms. That too she noticed right away. One time, when I stayed away for several days and then returned distraught, she took me aside and said: "You mustn't have wishes you don't believe in. I know what you wish for. Either you can give up these wishes or you need to fully and properly wish for them. If you can ever ask in such a way that you are entirely sure your wish will be fulfilled, then fulfillment will come. But now you're just wishing and then feeling bad about it, scared the whole time. That is what you need to overcome. Let me tell you a story."

And she told me that once upon a time there was a young man in love with a star in the sky. He stood on the ocean's shore, reached out his hands, and worshipped the star; he dreamed about it and directed all his thoughts at it. But he knew, or thought he knew, that a star cannot be clasped in human arms. He thought it was his destiny to love a heavenly body without any hope of fulfillment, and from this idea he constructed an entire poetry of life based on renunciation and silent faithful suffering that would make him purer and better. Still all his dreams were of the star. One night he was standing by the ocean again, on a high cliff, and he looked at the star and burned with love for it. And at the pinnacle of his greatest longing, he leaped into thin air toward the star. But the instant he made the leap, he thought, fast as lightning: It's not possible! Then he was lying down on the beach, broken to pieces. He did not know how to love. If, at the moment he jumped, he had had the strength of soul to be firm and sure that his longing would be fulfilled, he would have flown up to the sky and become one with the star.

"Love cannot ask," she said, "or plead. Love must have the strength to reach certainty from within. Then one's love is no longer attracted, it attracts. Sinclair, your love is drawn to me. If it ever draws *me* to *it*, I will come. I don't want to do anyone a favor, I want to be won."

Another time, she told me a different fairy tale. There once was a lover who loved without hope. He withdrew completely into his heart and thought his love would consume him. He was lost to the world; he no longer saw the blue sky and the green forest, the stream did not murmur past for him, the harp did not sound, everything was gone, and he had grown poor and miserable. Still his love grew and grew, and he would have much rather died and withered away than give up on possessing the beautiful woman he loved. Then he felt how his love had turned everything else in his heart to ashes; his passion grew powerful; its force of attraction pulled and pulled, and the beautiful woman had no choice but to obey: she came to him, and he stood with outspread arms to draw her to him. But she, standing there before him, had been utterly transformed—he saw and felt with a shudder that he had drawn the whole lost world to him. It stood before him and gave itself to him, sky and forest and mountain stream, everything came to him fresh and magnificent, in new colors, and it belonged to him, spoke his language. Instead of winning just one woman, he had the whole world pressed to his heart; every star in the sky shone within him, sparkling with pleasure through his soul. — He had loved and had found himself in the process. Most people love only in order to lose themselves.

My love for Eve seemed like the only thing in my life. But every day it looked different. Sometimes I felt certain that my essential nature was not in fact struggling to reach her actual person, rather that she was only a symbol of what was inside me, trying only to lead me deeper into myself. The things she said often sounded like my own unconscious mind's answers to the burning questions I had. At other times there were moments when I was aflame with sensual desire next to her, and kissed things she had touched. Gradually my sexual and asexual love, reality and symbol, began to merge. Then, thinking about her in calm tranquility alone in my room, I sometimes seemed to feel her hand in mine, her lips on mine. Or else I would be with her, looking into her face, talking to her and hearing her voice, and I couldn't tell if she was even real or just a dream. I started to realize how a person can possess a love forever, immortally. I learned something new from reading a book and it was the exact same feeling as a kiss from Eve; she stroked my hair and smiled her fresh, sweet-smelling warmth at me and I had the same feeling as when I had made progress within myself. Everything that mattered to me, every part of my destiny, could take on her shape. She could turn into every one of my thoughts and vice versa.

I had to spend Christmas vacation with my parents, and I had been afraid of it because I thought it would be torture to be away from Eve for two weeks. But it was no such thing—it was wonderful to be at home and to think about her. When I returned to H., I stayed away from her house for another two days, savoring my security and my independence from her physical presence. I had dreams, too, in which my union with her took place in new, metaphorical ways. She was an ocean and I was a river pouring into her; she was a star and I was another star hurtling toward her, and we met, felt drawn to each other, stayed close to each other, and orbited blissfully around each other in tight, singing circles for all eternity.

I told her this dream the next time I visited her.

"That's a beautiful dream," she said quietly. "Make it come true!"

Early that spring there came a day I will never forget. I walked into the hall, where a window was open; a warm breeze wafted the thick smell of hyacinths through the house. Since no one was there, I went upstairs to Max Demian's study. I knocked lightly on the door and, as I habitually did, walked in without waiting for an answer.

The room was dark, all the curtains pulled shut. The door to a small side room where Max had set up a chemical laboratory was open, and from there came the bright white light of the spring sun shining through the rain clouds. I thought no one was in the room, and I pulled back a curtain.

Then I saw Max Demian sitting on a stool near the curtained window, hunched over and strangely altered. A feeling flashed through me like lightning: you've seen that before! His arms hung limp with his hands in his lap, his head hung slightly bent forward, and his face, with his eyes open, was dead and unseeing—a tiny glare of reflected light shone in the pupil of one eye, as though in a dead piece of glass. His wan face was as if turned in on itself, expressionless except for a horrible rigidity; it looked like an ancient, primitive animal mask at the gate of a temple. He did not seem to be breathing.

I felt a shudder of memory: I had seen him like that, exactly like that, once before, many years ago, when I was still a boy. His eyes had stared inward the same way; his hands had lain lifelessly next to each other the same way; a fly had walked across his face. And back then, maybe six years before, he had looked exactly as old and as timeless as he looked now. Not a wrinkle in his face was any different.

Gripped with fear, I quietly left the room and went downstairs. In the hall I saw Eve. She looked pale and seemed tired, in a way I had never seen her. A shadow flew in through the window; the glaring white sunlight was suddenly gone.

"I just saw Max," I whispered hurriedly. "Has something happened? He is asleep, or turned in on himself, I don't know how to put it. I've seen him like that once before."

"You didn't wake him up, did you?" she asked hurriedly.

"No. He didn't hear me. I left right away. Tell me, Eve, what's the matter with him?"

She wiped her brow with the back of her hand.

"Don't worry, Sinclair, nothing's the matter with him. He has withdrawn. It won't last long."

She stood up and went out into the garden, even though it had just started to rain. I could tell I wasn't supposed to go with her. So I paced back and forth in the hall, smelled the stupefying scent of the hyacinths, stared at my bird picture over the door, and anxiously breathed in the strange shadow that had filled the house that morning. What was it? What had happened?

Eve soon came back. There were raindrops in her dark hair. She sat down in her armchair, exhausted. I walked over to her, bent down, and kissed the drops from her hair. Her eyes were quiet and bright, but the drops tasted like tears.

"Should I check on him?" I asked in a whisper.

She smiled weakly.

"Don't be a little boy, Sinclair!" she warned, in a loud voice as though trying to break a spell she was under. "Go away now, and come back later, I can't talk to you right now."

I left the house and hurried out of the city toward the mountains, into the fine, slanting rain. The clouds moved past, low in the sky, under heavy pressure, as though in fear; beneath them there was hardly any breeze. A storm seemed to be raging on the peaks. More than once the sun burst through the steel-gray clouds for a moment, pale in hue but dazzlingly bright.

Then a fluffy yellow cloud came drifting across the sky and crashed into the gray wall, collecting there. In a matter of seconds the wind had shaped a picture out of the yellow and the blue: a gigantic bird, tearing free from the chaos of blue and disappearing into the sky with great beats of its wings. All at once you could hear the storm, and rain beat down mixed with hail. A short clap of thunder, improbably and terrifyingly loud, burst across the landscape whipped with rain, and immediately the sun broke through the clouds again, and the pale snow glowed wan and unreal on the nearby mountains above the brown trees.

When I came back wet and pale, hours later, Demian himself opened the front door for me.

He took me up to his room. A gas flame was burning in his laboratory, and papers lay strewn about—he seemed to have been working.

"Sit down," he invited me. "You must be tired. The weather's terrible. You look like you really got caught outside. There'll be tea in a minute."

"Something strange is happening today," I hesitantly began. "It can't be just the weather."

He looked searchingly at me.

"Did you see something?"

"Yes. I saw a picture in the clouds for a moment. It was perfectly clear."

"What was it?"

"A bird."

"The sparrow hawk? Was it him? From your dream?"

"Yes, it was my hawk. It was yellow and gigantic and flew into the blue-black sky."

Demian heaved a great sigh.

There was a knock at the door. The old servant brought in the tea.

"Help yourself, Sinclair, please. . . . I think it was probably no accident that you saw the bird?"

"Accident? Does anyone see something like that by chance?"

"No, you're right. The bird means something. Do you know what it means?"

"No. I can only feel some kind of disruption, destiny taking another step. I think it has to do with us all."

He paced furiously back and forth.

"Destiny taking another step!" he cried. "Last night I dreamed the same thing, and my mother had a premonition yesterday with the same message. . . . I dreamed I was climbing up a ladder that was leaning against a tree trunk or tower. When I got to the top I saw the whole countryside on fire—a vast plain with cities and villages. I can't tell you everything, it's not all clear in my mind yet."

"Do you interpret the dream as being about you?" I asked.

"About me? Of course. No one dreams anything that has nothing to do with them. But it's not only about me, you're right. There's a pretty sharp distinction in my mind between the dreams that show movements in my own soul and the other, very rare dreams that point to a shift in the fate of all mankind. I have not had many of that second kind of dream, and not a single one I could call a prophecy that later came true. The interpretations are not that specific. But I know for certain that I've dreamed something not only about me, partly because it connects up with earlier dreams of mine, it continues them. These are the dreams that have given me the hunches I've talked to you about, Sinclair. We know that our world is rotten to the core, but that's not a sufficient reason to prophesy its decline or destruction or what have you. For the past several years, though, I have had dreams that make me conclude, or feel, or however you want to put it—that make me feel, then, that the collapse of the old world is approaching. At first they were very faint, distant intimations, but they have grown clearer and clearer, and stronger. I still don't know anything except that something major and terrible is coming, and that it will affect me. We are going to live through what we've talked about, Sinclair! The world wants to be reborn. The smell of death is in the air. Nothing new comes without death. . . . It's worse than I ever imagined." I stared at him in horror.

"You can't tell me the rest of your dream?" I asked shyly.

He shook his head.

"No."

The door opened. Eve walked in.

"There you two are! You're not sad, are you, children?"

She looked refreshed, no longer tired at all. Demian smiled at her, and she came up to us the way a mother comes to frightened children.

"We're not sad, Mother, we've just been trying to puzzle out something from these new signs. But it doesn't matter. Whatever it is that's about to happen will suddenly be here, and then we'll find out whatever we need to know."

But I was in a bad mood, and when I said goodbye and walked out through the hallway alone, the scent of the hyacinths seemed stale and cadaverous. A shadow had fallen over us.

CHAPTER EIGHT

THE BEGINNING
OF THE END

I had managed to get permission to stay in H— during the summer semester as well. We spent almost all our time not in the house but in the garden by the river. The Japanese man (who, incidentally, had lost decisively in the boxing match) was gone, the Tolstoyan too. Demian kept a horse and took long rides every day. I was often left alone with his mother.

I marveled sometimes at how peaceful my life was. I had spent so long in the habit of solitude, self-denial, and self-flagellation that those months in H— were like an enchanted dream island where I could live in comfort, and surrounded by nothing but beautiful, pleasant things and feelings. I could tell that this was a foretaste of the new, higher community we were imagining. Occasionally I would be seized with mourning for this happiness, since I knew full well it could not last. I was unable to breathe in an atmosphere of comfort and fullness—I needed torment and frenzy. I could feel that one day I would wake up out of this beautiful picture of love and happiness and stand alone once more, completely alone, in the cold world of other people, where my only choices were solitude or struggle—no peace, no shared life.

At these moments I would nestle up close to Eve with redoubled affection, glad that my destiny still wore this lovely, quiet face.

The summer weeks passed quickly and easily; the fall semester was already near. I was about to leave, I couldn't think about it—and I didn't think about it, instead I clung to these beautiful days like a butterfly to the honey clover. This had been my time of happiness, the first time in my life I had found fulfillment and been welcomed into a group of like-minded individuals. What would come next? I would carry on struggling, longing, dreaming, being alone.

I felt this premonition so strongly one day that my love for Eve suddenly flared up with painful intensity. My God, such a short time and then I would no longer see her, hear her firm, good footsteps walking through the house, find flowers from her on my table! And what had I accomplished? I had dreamed and wallowed in contentment instead of winning her, instead of fighting for her and making her mine forever! Everything she had ever told me about true love came rushing back to my mind—a hundred delicate warnings, a hundred gentle encouragements, maybe even promises—and what had I done with them? Nothing! Nothing!

I stood in the middle of my room, gathered all my mental energy, and thought about Eve. I wanted to summon up all the powers in my soul so that she would feel my love and be drawn to me. She *had* to come to me, had to long for my embrace; my kisses had to burrow insatiably into her ripe, loving lips.

I stood there and concentrated until my feet and fingers started to turn cold. I felt power radiating from me. For several moments something contracted inside me, firm and tight, something bright and cool: I felt for a second that I carried a crystal in my heart, and I knew that it was my Self. The coldness reached my chest.

When I emerged from this awful strain, I could feel that something was coming. I was dead tired, but ready to see Eve walk into the room, burning with rapture.

I heard hooves pounding up the long street, near and hard, and suddenly stopping. I sprang to the window. Demian was dismounting his horse downstairs. I ran down.

"What is it, Demian? Nothing's happened to your mother, has it?"

He did not seem to hear me. He was very pale and sweat ran

down his forehead over both cheeks; the horse was hot with effort too. Demian tied the reins to the garden fence, took my arm, and walked down the street with me.

"You've already heard?"

I hadn't heard anything.

Demian gripped my arm and turned his face to mine with a strange, dark, pitying look in his eyes.

"Yes, my boy, it's starting. You knew about the strained relations with Russia. . . ."

"What? Is it war? I never thought it would really—"

He spoke softly, even though no one was near: "It's not declared yet. But it's war. You can be sure of it. I didn't want to worry you since the last time, but I've seen three more signs since then. So it won't be an apocalypse, an earthquake, a revolution. It's war. And will it ever be popular! You'll see, Sinclair, it will be like a kind of mass insanity, already no one can wait to start fighting. Their lives have become so meaningless to them. . . . But you'll see, this is just the beginning. This may be a big war, a gigantic war, but even that is just the beginning. The new world is coming, horrific to anyone who clings to the old. — What are you going to do?"

I was confused, but it all still sounded so distant and improbable.

"I don't know. . . . You?"

He shrugged.

"I'll report for duty as soon as the mobilization comes. I'm a lieutenant."

"You? I had no idea!"

"Yes, it was one of the ways I conformed. You know how I don't like to stand out; I always preferred to go too far in the other direction, to seem proper. I'll be at the front by next week, I should think. . . ."

"For God's sake—"

"Well, my boy, don't be too sentimental about it. It won't be much fun to order artillery fire against other living human beings, but that's beside the point. Every one of us will be sucked into the system now. You too. You'll definitely be drafted."

"And your mother, Demian?"

Only then did I remember what had happened just a few minutes before. How the world had changed! I had exerted all my strength to summon up the sweetest of images, and now my destiny suddenly faced me in new form, wearing a threatening, horrific mask.

"My mother? Oh, you don't have to worry about her. She is safe, safer than anyone else in the world today. — Do you really love her that much?"

"You knew, Demian?"

He laughed a bright, free laugh.

"My dear boy! Of course I knew. No one has ever called my mother Eve without being in love with her. By the way, what just happened? You called her today, or me, didn't you?"

"Yes, I called — — I was calling Eve."

"She felt it. She abruptly sent me away and told me I had to go see you. I had just told her the news about Russia."

We turned back, talked a little more, then he untied his horse and mounted it.

Only when I got back upstairs to my room did I feel how exhausted I was, from Demian's news and much more from the effort that had come before. But Eve had heard me! I had reached her heart with my thoughts. She would have come herself, if not for — — How strange it all was, and, at bottom, how beautiful! So there would be war. Everything we had talked about so often was starting to happen. And Demian had foreseen so much of it. How strange, that the current of the world would no longer pass us by, somewhere else . . . instead it was suddenly running right through our hearts, adventures and wild fates were calling to us, and now, or soon, the moment would arrive when the world needed us, when it would be transformed. Demian was right: we shouldn't be sentimental about it. The only remarkable thing was that my "destiny," this private and solitary thing, would now be shared with so many other people, with the whole world, and that we would experience it together. Good!

I was ready. When I walked through the city that night, there was a buzz of great excitement on every corner. Wherever I turned, the word: "War"!

I went to Eve's house, and we ate in the summer house. I was the only guest that night. Neither of us said a word about the war. Only later, just before I left, did Eve say: "My dear Sinclair, you called me today. You know why I didn't come to you myself. But don't forget: Now you know the call, and whenever you need someone who bears the mark, use it again!"

She stood up and preceded me into the twilit garden. Tall and regal, full of mystery, she strode between the silent trees, and all the many stars shone tiny and delicate above her head.

I am coming to the end. Everything happened quite fast. The war started, and Demian, strangely unfamiliar in his uniform with the silver-gray overcoat, set out. I took his mother back to her house. Soon I said goodbye to her too; she kissed me on the mouth and hugged me to her breast for a moment, her large eyes blazing up close straight into mine.

And all people were as brothers. They thought it was the Fatherland, and Honor, but it was Fate whose unconcealed face they beheld for a moment. Young men emerged from their barracks and boarded trains, and on many of their faces I saw a sign—not ours, but a beautiful, dignified sign that meant love and death. I too was embraced by people I had never seen before, and I understood why, and happily responded in kind. It was a kind of intoxication that made them do it, not the will of their destiny, but that intoxication was holy too—it came from that short, thrilling look in the eye they had all given Fate.

It was almost winter when I arrived at the battlefield.

At first, despite all the excitement of gunfire, everything disappointed me. Earlier I had given much thought to why people were so rarely capable of living for an ideal; now I saw that many, indeed all people were capable of dying for one. Only it could not be a personal ideal, freely chosen; it had to be a common one, taken from someone else.

With time, though, I realized I had not given people enough credit. No matter how much their service and common danger made them all alike, I still saw many, many people, living and dying, who approached the will of fate with great dignity.

They had the steady, distant, almost possessed look of those who have completely surrendered to the unimaginable, who care nothing about the goal—and this not only while launching an attack, but all the time. Whatever they might think or believe, they were ready—they were of use—a future would grow from them. And the more fixated the world was on war, heroism, honor, and all the other old ideals, the more distant and improbable any voice of apparent humanity might sound, it was all on the surface, the same way the question of the external and political objectives of the war remained on the surface. Underneath, something was in the process of becoming. Something like a new humanity. For I saw many men, some of them dying at my side, who had arrived at the deeply felt insight that hate and anger, killing and destruction, were not connected to the objects of these actions and emotions. These objects, like the war's objectives, were entirely accidental. Primal emotions, even the most violent, were not intended for the enemy: their bloody work was merely an emanation from inside, a manifestation of the self-divided soul that wanted to rampage and kill, destroy and die, in order to be reborn. A giant bird was fighting its way out of the egg, and the egg was the world, and the world had to shatter to pieces.

One early spring night I was standing guard in front of a farmstead we had occupied. A listless wind blew in fitful gusts; armies of clouds rode high across the Flemish sky with somewhere behind them a hint of the moon. I had felt uneasy that whole day; something was worrying me. Now, at my dark post, I thought deeply about the images from my life thus far: about Eve, about Demian. I stood leaning against a poplar tree, and I gazed into the turbulent sky, where mysteriously shifting bright spots soon formed a large, surging series of images. From the strange weakness in my pulse, my skin's insensitivity to wind and rain, and my sparks of inner wakefulness, I could feel that a guide was near me.

I could see a giant city in the clouds, with millions of people streaming out of it and swarming across the vast countryside. In their midst a powerful goddess-figure appeared, as large as a mountain range, with glittering stars in her hair and with

Eve's features. The streams of people vanished into it as though into an enormous pit, and were gone. The goddess crouched on the ground and the mark on her brow glowed bright. She seemed in the grip of a dream: she closed her eyes, her huge face twisted in pain. Suddenly she shrieked, and stars leaped out of her brow, thousands of shining stars hurtling in magnificent arcs and semicircles across the black sky.

One of the stars shot straight at me with a shriek; it seemed to be trying to find me. . . . Then it burst apart, screaming, into a thousand sparks, flinging me up and then throwing me back to the ground. The world collapsed in thunder above me.

They found me near the poplar, covered with earth and with many wounds.

I was in a cellar with shots whizzing overhead. I was lying in a wagon, bumping across empty fields. Most of the time I was asleep, or unconscious. But the deeper into my sleep I went, the more violently I felt something drawing me on—that I was obeying a power that was my master.

I was lying in a stable, on straw. It was dark and someone had stepped on my hand. But something inside me wanted me to keep going, and pulled me more strongly than ever. Again I was in a wagon, later on a stretcher or ladder. I felt summoned somewhere more and more powerfully, felt nothing but the need to finally get there.

Then I had arrived. It was night, I was fully conscious, and I had just felt the pull and need inside me with extra force. Now I was lying in a large room, bedded down on the floor, and I felt I was where I had been summoned to. I looked around. Another mattress lay right next to mine with someone on it, who leaned over and looked at me. He had the mark on his forehead. It was Max Demian.

I couldn't speak, and he couldn't either, or didn't want to. He just looked at me. The light from a bulb hanging on the wall above him shone on his face. He smiled at me.

He kept looking into my eyes for an endless length of time. Then he slowly brought his face closer to me until we almost touched.

"Sinclair!" he said in a whisper.

I signaled with my eyes that I could hear him.

He smiled again, almost as though in pity.

"Little friend!" he said, smiling.

His mouth was now very close to mine. He softly went on: "Do you still remember Franz Kromer?" he asked.

I blinked at him and managed to smile too.

"Listen, little Sinclair! I have to go away. You may need me again someday, against Kromer or something else. The next time you call me, I won't come so obviously on horseback or by train. You will have to listen inside yourself, and then you'll realize I'm in you. Do you understand? . . . One more thing! Eve said if you're ever in trouble, I should give you the kiss from her she sent with me. Close your eyes, Sinclair!"

I obediently closed my eyes and felt a light kiss on my lips, where I still had a little blood that refused to ever go away. Then I fell asleep.

Someone woke me up the next morning to be bandaged. When at last I was fully awake, I turned quickly to the neighboring mattress. On it was lying a stranger I had never seen before.

The bandaging hurt. Everything that has happened to me since has hurt. But sometimes, when I find the key and climb fully down into myself, where the images of destiny slumber in their dark mirror, I need only bend down over the black mirror and I see my own image, which now looks exactly like Him, Him, my friend and my guide.

AVAILABLE FROM PENGUIN CLASSICS

Siddhartha

ISBN 978-0-14-243718-6

PENGUIN
CLASSICS

Hermann Hesse's
Siddhartha is perhaps the most
important and compelling
moral allegory the 20th century
ever produced. Integrating
Eastern and Western spiritual
traditions with psychoanalysis
and philosophy, this strangely
simple tale, written with a
deep and moving empathy for
humanity, has touched the lives
of millions since its original
publication in 1922. This
Penguin Classics Deluxe Edition
of Hesse's beloved novel features
Joachim Neugroschel's stunning
translation and an indispensable
introductory essay by
Ralph Freedman, Hesse's
definitive biographer.